GIRL UPSIDE DOWN

GIRL
UPSIDE
DOWN

NICOLE WILLIAMS

CROWN 👑 New York

Text copyright © 2019 by Nicole Williams

All rights reserved. Published in the United States by
Crown Books for Young Readers,
an imprint of Random House Children's Books,
a division of Penguin Random House LLC, New York.

Crown and the colophon are registered trademarks
of Penguin Random House LLC.

Visit us on the Web! GetUnderlined.com

Educators and librarians, for a variety of teaching tools, visit us at
RHTeachersLibrarians.com

Library of Congress Cataloging-in-Publication Data is available upon request.
ISBN 978-0-553-49885-1 (trade pbk.) — ISBN 978-0-553-49887-5 (ebook)

Cover design by Casey Moses
Cover photo of girl © BONNIN-STKOID/Stocksy United

Printed in the United States of America
10 9 8 7 6 5 4 3 2 1
First Edition

Random House Children's Books
supports the First Amendment and celebrates the right to read.

To the bookworms. My people. My tribe.
You make this book world a happy, beautiful place.

To my dearest, Quinn,

some words of wisdom—I see that eye roll, but just trust me!—to get you through these next few years. Miss you already.

Love,

Mom

*The upside to hitting rock bottom is
that there's only one direction left to go.

Up.*

Life wasn't a fairy tale. Fifteen years in, and I already knew that.

In my experience, life was the opposite—instead of chasing a happy ending, it was more about keeping the unhappy one from nipping at your heels.

I wondered if other kids who'd lost a parent felt the same way.

As the bus pulled into the depot, my fingers curled around the worn suede journal I'd been clutching since boarding in Leavenworth, Washington, aka the only home I'd ever known and now had no clue when I'd ever see again.

Renton might have been in the same state, but it wasn't anything like the place where I'd spent my whole life. A suburb of Seattle, Renton appeared to be as packed with cars, people, and urban sprawl as the Emerald City.

When the announcement screeched through the bus speakers that we'd arrived at the Seattle bus depot, I was the only person not in a hurry to get off. After breathing in a few hours of stale air and suspicious body odors, you'd think I'd be elbowing my way down the aisle with the rest of them, but what was waiting for me out there was more terrifying than anything inside this bus.

A new life.

One I hadn't chosen but was instead forced into thanks to being a minor and low on alternatives. In a little over two years, I'd be of legal age and able to call the shots when it came to my life, but in the meantime, I was stuck with him.

Him.

I couldn't bring myself to say the name I'd called him the first five years of my life. I wasn't sure I ever would. Kind of hard to call someone Dad when he bailed forever ago and hadn't made contact since.

Why did Mom leave me in his custody instead of someone else's? I asked myself for the millionth time as I tucked the journal into my shoulder bag and forced myself up from the seat. After the doctors told Mom the grim news of how much—or how little—time she had left, she filled the journal with wisdom and advice for me. I'd seen her working on it those last weeks we had together, but it wasn't until after her death that one of her friends gave it to me. I'd been savoring every passage, every *word*, since and was dreading reaching the end.

I was now officially the last one on the bus and making no

move to hustle off either. While other passengers were lined up outside, waiting to claim their bags, I bit back every urge and instinct to tear over to the ticket counter and purchase a one-way back to Leavenworth.

Home. Friends. *Belonging.*

I could live on my own, find a job, and finish school there. It would be hard—I knew that—but it would be a picnic compared to whatever life waited for me here.

I'd checked into it. Emancipation.

The paperwork, the ins and outs; I knew about all of it. I also knew enough to decide I wasn't quite ready for that big of a step. Not yet. I'd give this new living situation a trial period before making up my mind. If it sucked as bad as I'd been guessing it would, emancipation it would be. Plus my mom had wanted this: me to come live with Nick. If nothing else, I was going to honor her wishes and give it a chance.

Climbing off the bus, I could already feel the moisture in the air. Only a hundred miles away and I'd gone from four distinct seasons to one: rain.

I concentrated on finding my luggage instead of scanning the depot for him. He'd left a voice message for me a couple of days ago saying he'd pick me up when my bus arrived at four-thirty. He'd offered to drive me from Leavenworth to save me the headache of the bus, but being trapped in a confined space for two and a half hours with the man who walked out on me and Mom sounded a hundred times worse than any bus ride.

Finally, I spotted my bags and slung the two duffels over my shoulders. I took a moment to put on the most unaffected face I could before turning around to where a handful of people were waiting for passengers. I hadn't seen him in a decade, and I wondered if I'd even recognize him now.

Of course, he looked almost exactly the same.

I'd been in kindergarten the last time he saw me, though. My hair had gone from white to dark blond, I'd grown a solid foot and a half, and I'd ditched the dresses for jeans and T-shirts. Not to mention that the innocent twinkle in my eyes was long gone. A result of having one parent bail and the other lose her life to a bastard of a disease.

I kept my gaze wandering and tucked my hoodie up over my head as I started toward him, not about to give him the wrong impression that I was thrilled with this arrangement.

This wasn't a happy reunion. It wasn't a long overdue visit.

This was his guilt and my helplessness colliding.

This was my proverbial rock and a hard place.

He teetered on the curb as I approached, each step harder to take than the one before.

It wasn't until I'd stopped on the curb semi-beside him, arms crossed and eyes still roaming, that he seemed to recognize me and unfroze from his statue-like state. Clearing his throat, he began to stretch his arms as his body squared toward me. Almost as if he was about to give me a . . .

I backed away a few feet. Then one more just in case.

His arms hung in the air for a brief second before falling to his sides.

Seriously, though. Did he just expect I'd be all for hugging it out? It wasn't like he'd stayed late at work one night and missed my school recital or something. He'd left me. He'd left *us*.

If he thought some awkward hug was the solution to a

decade-long absence, I was going to need that emancipation quicker than I'd guessed.

"I'm sorry, Quinn." The first words I'd heard from my "dad" in years settled into the space between us. His voice was a bit deeper than I remembered, grittier. "I'm so sorry."

It was probably the thousandth time I'd heard that sentiment since Mom had died. You'd have thought I'd be desensitized to those words by now, but not even close. Blinking my eyes to keep the sting in them from materializing, I cleared my throat. "Where did you park?"

He stood there for another minute, shifting his weight from foot to foot like he wanted to say something else, but all that came was a long sigh. "This way."

He pointed in the general direction of the parking lot behind the terminal, and we started moving. As soon as I left the shelter, raindrops began to pepper me. It wasn't a hard rain, but instead the unhurried kind that made it known it wasn't planning on stopping anytime this month.

I'd never been big on rain. Sure, Seattle rain might have been responsible for flowers blooming, but it was also responsible for spirits withering. I could already feel mine dwindling as my sneakers clomped around the shallow puddles scattered through the parking lot.

"This is me." His head lifted at the familiar old truck in front of us.

My stomach seized seeing it again, an image playing through my head of its taillights fading from view as the miniature version of me stood crying on a sidewalk.

"Let me get those." When he started to reach for my bags after opening the creaky passenger door, I flinched away.

"I've got it, Nick."

Calling him by his name surprised me, but from his expression, it didn't surprise him. Backing away, he moved around the bed to the driver's side, while I finished wrestling my bags into the back seat. The truck was already running by the time I crawled into the passenger seat, the engine gasping for air. The windows fogged up from the rain, and the heaters created a sauna-like feel inside the cab.

"You've grown up. Changed so much since the last time I saw you," Nick said as we left the bus parking lot.

"That's what happens when a decade goes by," I replied, angling toward my window. I wasn't in a talking mood.

He must have picked up on what I was getting at, because he didn't say anything else the rest of the drive. In the silence, I tried to acquaint myself with my new home. My new *residence*, I reminded myself, because this would never be home.

Endless green, gray, and people—that's what this place was made of. It was all so different from where I'd grown up. It was hard to imagine a place that could be more different. The sun had been shining when I'd left Leavenworth. Here it seemed like the sun hadn't made an appearance in months.

The sun.

Just one of the many things I'd have to learn to go without here in purgatory.

"Still follow baseball?" Nick asked suddenly, making an attempt to fill in the silence.

I cringed at the question. Baseball was the one thing we ever had in common. "When I have the time," I replied coldly.

His face pinched together like he was trying to think of what to say next. Luckily, after a minute, he gave it up.

Almost an hour had gone by, most of that time spent stuck in traffic, before we pulled onto a side street speckled with houses and apartments. It was an old part of town, some buildings maintained, some not so much.

"Here we are," Nick announced as he eased the truck up to the curb in front of a small apartment complex.

I took in a breath before letting myself see the place I'd potentially be spending the next two years of my life. It wasn't the worst I'd imagined . . . but it was a long way off from the best.

I unbuckled and leapt from the truck. I already had my bags shouldered by the time Nick came around to meet me on the sidewalk.

He must have noticed the way I was gaping at the small complex, because he motioned at the building. "I know it's not much to look at, but the apartments are clean and rent doesn't cost an arm and a leg."

My throat constricted as my gaze continued to wander the lava rock structure that appeared as though nothing had been updated since the seventies.

"It's . . ." I struggled to substitute a word that wouldn't totally offend him. "*Nice.*"

"It's nicer on the inside, trust me," he replied, leading the way up the sidewalk to the main entrance.

I followed, feeling like I was walking the plank instead of entering my new "home."

"There are only six apartments, mainly filled with older folks, so it's pretty quiet, which will be nice for you when it comes time to study." He led the way up a stairway. "And the high school is only half a mile away, so you can either take the bus or walk to school, you know, at least until you get your license."

"That's . . . nice," I repeated, filing that response away for future reference. Didn't express enthusiasm but wasn't insulting either. Exactly the line I wanted to straddle where Nick was concerned.

"Yeah. Nice." He rubbed at the back of his head as he pulled a set of keys from his pocket. It was so strange to see him with streaks of gray hair popping through the dark strands. He was still tall and thin, like he could have stood to gain ten pounds, his wiry beard the same as before, but he'd changed a little too. He appeared tired, almost fragile compared to the younger version of him I remembered.

We stopped in front of an apartment on the second floor, a number five hanging crookedly on the door. It was in need of a fresh coat of paint, ten years ago. The smell lingering in the hallway was musty, like years of rain had been collecting inside the worn wood floors.

"This is us." For the first time, Nick's voice sounded unsteady. "It isn't much, but it's home." He moved aside, letting me pass through first.

Which was a good thing, since I couldn't hide the surprise that hit me the moment I stepped into the apartment.

It was all one big room, from what I could tell; the kitchen, dining, living room all gelling into one.

"This is it?" My voice wobbled. "Where are the bedrooms?"

The clearing of his throat as he came inside answered my question. Mostly. "My bedroom's right over there, by the bathroom." He waved at one corner of the apartment, where a couple of dark doorways stood.

"And my bedroom?"

I saw it right before he angled toward it: the cluster of curtains that had been hung from the ceiling, partitioning off a small corner of the room.

"This is only temporary. Until I can find us a bigger place." Nick pulled one of the curtains aside, revealing my new "bedroom." Inside, a small bed had been squeezed, along with a few plastic rolling carts that I assumed were meant to serve as my dresser and closet.

There was a floor lamp, a small purple rug to match the comforter set, and a mismatch of purple curtains he'd hung to create an illusion of privacy. Purple had been my favorite color as a kid.

It had been my least favorite color for a while now.

He rubbed at the back of his head again, watching me take in the space. "Probably not what you're used to—"

"It's nice." I began taking the bags off my shoulders, setting them on the whole foot and a half of space I had to move around in my "room." "If you don't mind, I'd like to get unpacked and settled in."

I didn't wait for him to leave before tearing open the zipper of my first duffel. Good thing I hadn't brought a lot with me—I'd be lucky to fit what I had into the plastic drawers. One of my friends' parents had offered to keep the rest of Mom's and my stuff in their garage, saying it would be there for me one day whenever I needed it.

Another wave of homesickness bowled over me.

"If you need anything, let me know." He went to leave, letting the curtain close behind him. "I'll give you some privacy."

I needed to cry. I needed to scream. But I had walls of

cotton and nowhere to run to. Collapsing on the foam bed, I felt the tears come on their own. In the span of a handful of days, I'd lost my mom, my friends, my home—my whole life. And I couldn't help thinking I no longer had anyone to cry to.

Find the good.

One night down. Only eight hundred and something more to go.

A grumble escaped from me when I thought about it in those terms.

Find the good.

Mom had a lot of words of wisdom when it came to winning at life—a result of all those self-improvement books, I suppose—but that was her favorite: Find the good, and you'll deflect the bad.

And for the most part, it worked. Even the time I'd gotten sick and had to miss the sixth-grade camping trip I'd been excited for all year. Mom turned the living room into the great outdoors, complete with sleeping bags, lanterns, and hanging stars. We finished off each night with s'mores roasted over the stove.

The good then was easy to find: I got to spend a special weekend with my mom. *But now?* I thought, scanning my bedroom made of mismatched curtains and yellowed water stains dotting the ceiling, it seemed impossible to find.

My alarm went off a minute later. It was my first day at my new high school, and as much as I didn't want to go, Mom had pounded enough sense into me to know school was important. She said college was up to me, but it was her job to make sure I made it through high school.

Even though she wasn't here, I felt like I couldn't let her down. So after "owning my brave" (another Mom-ism), I'd almost made my escape—showered, dressed, and ready for school—when I heard the bedroom door creak open.

I should have kept going, pretending I hadn't noticed, but for some stupid reason, I paused in the doorway, waiting.

"You're leaving early." His voice was thick with sleep as he hurried across the apartment toward the kitchen. "Let me make you some breakfast before you take off. Most important meal of the day." He was still dressed in what he'd been wearing last night. Maybe he hadn't slept or maybe he slept in his clothes, but I wasn't about to ask. Questions showed interest, which expressed concern—I didn't have those feelings for him, I reminded myself.

I busied myself with the zipper of my hoodie. "I already ate."

Nick spun a couple of circles in the kitchen, like he didn't have a clue what to make for breakfast.

"I've got to get going. I don't want to be late," I added as he began searching through cupboards as though they might have magically been stocked overnight by the grocery fairy.

"School doesn't start until eight-fifteen." His attention flickered to the clock on the stove. "It's not even seven."

"It's my first day. I need to get my schedule, find my locker, figure out where my classes are, that kind of stuff." Not to mention a few million other things I'm sure I hadn't even thought of. "Really, I'm good. But thanks," I added when he retrieved a box of microwave popcorn from the cupboard above the fridge.

Last night's dinner had consisted of a frozen pizza he'd foraged from the ice-encrusted depths of the freezer. It had tasted more freezer than pizza. I'd be leery of anything that came from that kitchen from now on, even a bag of Jiffy Pop.

"Then, here. Take this." After stuffing the popcorn back in the cupboard, he opened the fridge and took out a brown bag. "I packed you a lunch." He held the brown bag toward me, taking me by surprise. My name was even penned across the front.

I guessed it contained the leftovers of the pizza, but taking it seemed like the quickest way to escape. "Thanks," I said as I stuffed the paper sack into my backpack. "I'll see you after school." As I moved into the hallway, I paused, scheming on the quick. "I'll probably be home late. I'm going to stay to finish my homework and use the Wi-Fi at school to check out some stuff." Another obstacle toward "finding the good"? No Wi-Fi in the prison known as this apartment. Which cut me off that much more from my old life, since my cell phone plan had been slashed down to the bare bones in those last few months. Money had been tight

15

with all the medical bills, and cell phones, contrary to popular belief, were a luxury when it was between that and keeping the lights on.

" 'Some stuff'?" Nick echoed, trying his hand at being parental. About ten years too late.

With Mom, I would have caved and spilled everything I had planned for the afternoon detail by detail, but with him . . .

"I'll see you later," I said quietly, continuing toward the stairs. I was half expecting him to come after me, demanding to know what I meant by *some stuff* and how late *late* was, but he never did. The door whined closed behind me.

There was a smidgeon of good, at least. Nick wasn't in the business of helicopter parenting, and I was going to take advantage of that. I had every intention of filling my waking hours with life outside that apartment, away from him.

As soon as I moved outdoors, I realized my mistake. I hadn't thought to grab my umbrella or my raincoat. Instead of retracing my steps, I soldiered onto the wet sidewalk and got moving. It could have been a torrential downpour and I wouldn't have headed back into that apartment. The school was impossible to miss, Nick had said. Turn left outside the apartment and follow a straight line until a giant high school appeared.

The rain made the trip faster than I estimated it would take, so Riverview High barely appeared awake by the time the sidewalk spit me out in front of the sprawling mass that just as easily could have been mistaken for a condemned hospital. Gray, blocky, and sterile. That was my first impression of my new school. It couldn't have been any more different from my old school if it tried. . . .

Right up until I made it through the heavy front doors and was greeted by a blockade of metal detectors and security guards.

So I guess it could be more different.

After setting my backpack on the scanner's conveyor belt, I waited to be motioned through the metal detector. Thank god it didn't beep, because getting wanded by a dude who gave off the vibe that his sole purpose was to intimidate teenagers was not the way I wanted to kick off the year at my new school.

As soon as my bag cleared the scanner, I snagged it and trudged down the hall in search of the office. My soaking shoes squeaked along the floor. I could have used a map, because this place seemed to be a maze of halls and rooms. Nick had already taken care of the initial registration stuff, but the next two years and change of adjusting to a new high school was on me.

The office was almost as quiet as the rest of the school, but there was one lady who was working behind her desk, who noticed me—or more likely my noisy shoes—when I approached. She appeared surprised to see me. When she checked the standard school clock hanging on the wall across from her, she looked even more so.

"Can I help you, hon?" she asked, setting her oversized coffee cup on the desk.

"This is my first day, and I think I'm supposed to get my schedule here."

She shot me a sympathetic smile, like this development was something to be pitied. "Name?"

"Quinn Winters."

She pounded the keys at the old school computer. "Ah,

there you are." She punched one last key. "I'll print your schedule and locker assignment, and you'll be all set."

Right. Because that's all it takes to fit in at a new school.

"Thanks," I said when she handed the paperwork to me. I gave it a quick check. Similar classes to what I was taking at my last school, just different times. My nose wrinkled when I read what was listed for first period: PE.

Not only was PE the universe's way of tormenting me, I had the added misfortune of being forced to suffer through it during the first class of the day. So I could wander the halls the rest of the day as a stinky, wilted mess.

"If you need anything else, just stop by. Okay, hon?"

What if I need a brand-new life?

I assumed she meant adding money to my lunch card or turning in an excuse note, though, so I kept that to myself.

"Oh," I said, remembering as I turned to leave. "Do you have a map? This place is bigger than my last school."

By about ten times.

"It might seem confusing, but it's really a big square. If you get lost, just keep going and you'll eventually get there." She passed me a photocopied map, her smile tipping into the sympathetic realm again. "Good luck."

The way she said it made it seem like I was shipping to the front lines, which did nothing to calm my nerves. Nothing like starting a megaschool in the middle of the school year as a sophomore.

Giving the map a quick check, I headed down the hall to where the library was supposed to be if the map was to be trusted. My soggy Birkenstocks echoing through the empty halls. The rest of my outfit, along with my hair, was just as wet. I would not forget that umbrella tomorrow.

18

Entering the library as a drenched poodle, I found it as empty as the rest of the school. The lights were still off. If I hadn't triple-checked the school calendar last week, I would have thought it was a teacher workday. Classes began in forty-five minutes and the place was a graveyard.

The computers lining a couple of long tables in the middle were powered off, but I couldn't imagine any self-respecting librarian would mind if I turned one on for "research" purposes.

Heading toward them, I flipped on the overhead lights. They flickered to life, humming as light burst through the room. I'd taken only a few steps when I heard something stirring from the back of the room.

"Who turned on the lights?" an irritated grumble echoed from the far corner.

Craning my neck, I could just make out some movement in the periodicals section of the library. "I did."

"Then you better turn them back off, Idid."

I sidestepped over so I had a better view of what appeared to be someone getting up from the floor, almost like he'd been perusing the magazines on his stomach. Or, more likely, taking a nap.

His back was to me, but he didn't look like a student. Despite the jeans and T-shirt that were two sizes too big for him, he was still two sizes bigger than the average high school boy. Maybe the librarian? No, didn't even come close to fitting that mold. Maybe the custodian?

Oh, wait. No. I already knew who the school custodian was.

"What are you doing in here?" I asked as he rolled his neck a couple of times.

"It's the library. What everyone does in this place." His wide shoulders rose beneath the white tee as he turned in my direction. He might have looked like an adult from the back, but he looked like a teen from the front. Just barely, though.

"Study?" I guessed as he moved closer.

He shot me a funny expression. "Sleep," he replied, his voice groggy.

"Why were you sleeping in the library?" I held my place, crossing my arms, fighting the instinct to retreat from him. He didn't exactly scream danger—it was more of a whisper.

"Because it was dark and quiet. Before you arrived, at least." He paused when he was still a distance away from me, almost like he was used to people needing their space where he was concerned.

I wasn't sure what to say, so I stared instead. In my defense, he was the kind of guy who was hard not to stare at. Brownish, messy hair, dark, restless eyes, and a mouth carved into a perma-smirk. Easy on the eyes and hard on the respiratory system.

"Okay, and clearly you're not getting the hint, so I'll be on my way to the next quiet, dark hole in this place." As he moved toward the exit, he kept that measured distance from me. "You on the swim team or something?"

My forehead creased. "No."

"You're soaked head to toe. Looks like you've just been in a pool."

I stabbed my finger in the direction of a couple of windows, getting the feeling this guy was having too much fun at my expense. "Rain."

"You know what part of the country you're in, right?"

When he gave half a smile, I could see the faintest gap between his top teeth. "Maybe you really do need this library more than I do." Waving in the general direction of the middle of the library, he backed away through the door. "Geography is somewhere in that section. Start there, then maybe finish with a trip to the store for some rain gear. You know, unless showing up to school every day looking like you're training for the summer Olympics is your thing."

I was struggling to form a comeback when he thumped the poster hanging above the door. "Make today great, Idid," he recited in the most sarcastic tone I had yet to hear.

My comeback finally came a minute later. A pathetic reply of "My name's not Idid."

When you're upset, just imagine
a T. rex trying to make a bed.
You're welcome.

*T*he rest of the day went like the morning—rough.

The highlight so far was that I'd mostly dried out by the time third period finished.

I settled on a table toward the front of the room, the emptiest by far. I'd never sat down to a school lunch alone before. Not once. But there were lots of firsts I was getting used to in this new life that had been carved out for me. In the scheme of things, sitting like a loner through a lunch wasn't that bad.

Unzipping my bag, I freed the brown paper lunch sack Nick had insisted I take. I dumped the contents on the table. It wasn't frozen pizza, but it was still a good thing I wasn't hungry.

Beef jerky, a handful of some large nut that was still in the shell (pretty sure a plastic knife wasn't up to the task of cracking open one of those babies), and finally, a bag of fruit snacks. Definitely not your typical lunch fare.

I started to toss it all back into the bag, but as I was throwing in the fruit snacks, something made me pause. The brand was familiar. They were the same kind I'd loved as a kid. In the shape of X's and O's. I remembered being able to sucker Mom or Nick into playing a game or two before wolfing them down.

I hadn't had any since Mom read an article about high fructose corn syrup eight years ago and our cupboards had never been the same since. X's and O's. How was that for coincidence that the snacks had wound up in my lunch today?

I wasn't sure Nick would recall the color of my eyes if I wasn't standing in front of him in bright light, so they had to be a random fluke. I popped one of the familiar gummy X's into my mouth before tossing the rest.

By the time sixth-period chemistry started, I felt like I really had gone to war. At least the high school equivalent.

As was the trend for the day, I'd crossed the threshold just as the final bell was finishing. Seriously, sprinting between classes should have counted toward my PE credit.

The teacher was typing at his computer, so I seized his distraction to glide onto the closest empty stool I could find. Maybe he'd take mercy on me and save the introduction hell.

"In case you all missed that blaring sound just now, that was the bell, which means that for the next fifty-five minutes, your undivided attention is mine." He glanced up from the desktop. The first place his eyes went was toward me.

"We have a new student in class."

I slumped on my stool, wincing from the inevitable.

"I trust you'll show her the same amount of respect and concern you show me." He paused, eyeing the handful of cell phones still in hands and conversations scattered around the room. "Oh wait. I take that back. I trust you'll show her the respect and concern you fail to show me to any regular degree."

That got a slight reaction from the class, most of the students tucking their phones into their pockets or backpacks, most of the conversations coming to an end as well.

"Ah, that's the trick. Nothing like a little self-deprecation to get your attention."

An actual laugh echoed through the room.

"For those of you who are new or new to tuning in to your esteemed teacher, I'm Mr. Johnson."

From the back of the room a one-off snort-laugh.

"Ah, yes, Ethan. Never gets old when I announce my last name to a classroom of teenagers. It's my way of distinguishing the mature ones from the others." Mr. Johnson adjusted his plaid bow tie, moving toward the whiteboard. "Of course, you'd think two misfortunately last named individuals would stick together. Wouldn't you, Mr. Wiener?"

This time it was a definite burst of laughter. No muffled ones this round.

"You're in my seat."

I flinched first from the surprise, then again when I saw who it was standing beside my lab table. "It doesn't have your name on it." I gazed up front, pretending to be fascinated by whatever Mr. Johnson was going on about.

For our teacher's part, he didn't seem to notice that a student had just trudged in late and said student was trying to intimidate me from my stool.

"This is my seat."

I kept my attention on the whiteboard, though it wasn't easy. Not with a particularly cute, massively huge guy hovering a few feet away.

"Are they assigned?" I said.

"It is for me," he replied, slipping off his backpack and dropping it on the floor beside me.

"That sounds like a no. Find another spot. Or are you some kind of troublemaker? Gotta sit up front where the teacher can see you?"

Instead of pressing the issue any longer, he snagged an empty stool and scooted it toward the table. "It's been determined that I fit into the category of Does Not Play Well with Others."

"In case *you* didn't notice, I fall into the category of 'others.'" I moved farther down the table; more distance was better where this guy was concerned.

Those dark eyes skimmed over me from the side, a crooked smile falling into place. "Consider me a skeptic, Idid."

"That's not my name."

"Whatever you say," he replied, turning his attention to Mr. Johnson, who was diving into a quick review of the periodic table.

"Would you please just leave me alone?"

He folded his arms over the table and rested his chin on them. "You got it, Idid."

Biting my tongue, I swallowed my reply.

"The element for chemical symbol 'A-S.'" Mr. Johnson circled his finger in the air before pointing it in the direction of a corner of the room. "Miss Fallon. 'A-S.'"

"Miss Fallon" had this put-out scowl on her face.

She glimpsed at the periodic table.

"I don't know. Hydrogen," she replied in a bored voice, smacking loudly on her gum.

Mr. Johnson sighed. "That answer makes me question my life's work, Miss Fallon. Congratulations."

She rolled her eyes while Mr. Johnson set his sights on the next student. The one sitting beside me.

"Mr. Remington. 'A-S.'" Mr. Johnson braced himself for another answer of the helium or silver caliber.

"Arsenic."

Mr. Johnson's face went blank for a moment. "That's correct. And thank you, Mr. Remington, for reaffirming my life's calling. Albeit temporarily, until one of you answers 'C-A' with 'California.' Isn't that right, Mr. Schroder?"

A student with a sideways baseball cap gave a little bow while his surrounding classmates chuckled.

The rest of the class went the same way. Mr. Johnson hammered in as much information as possible with wry humor and spouts of laughter mixed in between. I'd taken my notebook, but at the end of the period, all I'd written down was the date. I'd learned the periodic table at the beginning of the year at my old school.

My other classes had been the same. All reviews of

26

material I'd gone over months ago. If today was any indication of how the rest of my days would go in my new hood, I
was in serious danger of death by boredom.

Contrary to my suspicions, "Mr. Remington" left me
alone for the rest of class. I don't think he'd spared one
glimpse my way. His biggest response all period after that
one correct answer.

When the bell rang, I gathered up my things, feeling the
teensiest bit bad for being so snappy with him. He was one
of the only students who'd acknowledged my existence
today, after all.

"Nice work on the arsenic guess," I said, daring a sideways peek.

He was still on the stool, unlike the rest of the students
charging through the door. "It wasn't a guess."

My cheeks heated when I realized how I'd worded it. "I
didn't mean—"

"I *know* toxic." His dark eyes found mine for the briefest
moment before he rose from his seat. Instead of jetting for
the exit, he seemed to be stalling at the edge of the table. Like
he was waiting for someone. Me?

"Well, you gave one of the two right answers today," I said.

"And you gave the other."

Once I threw on my backpack and came around the table,
he started to move, still careful to keep some measured space
between us.

"What's your name?" I asked, feeling strange that we'd
already exchanged insults and a couple of conversations, and
were now possibly making amends, but we didn't actually
know each other's names.

27

"Other than Mr. Remington?"

"Yeah, that's weird. Does Mr. Johnson always do that?"

He nodded as we moved down the hall. "I think he hopes that by calling us Mr. or Miss, we'll eventually start behaving like adults instead of kids."

"Any progress with that?"

"You just sat through class, right? What do you think?"

I could feel a smile wanting to form and the lightness it generated inside. "So? Name? Because I'm not going to call you Mr. Remington."

One corner of his mouth twitched. "You *just* called me Mr. Remington."

"I'm about to call you Mr. Butthole if you don't answer the question."

He smiled, and I noticed a faint bruise on his cheek.

"Well, that's one of the nicer things I've been called," he said.

I groaned as we continued down the busy hall, and I didn't miss the way the crowds seemed to part as we moved through them. I knew from earlier that this had nothing to do with me, which meant it had everything to do with him. In the same way he kept me at a distance, the rest of the school seemed to pay him the same respect.

It was kind of eerie moving down a crowded hall and watching it open up as we passed through.

"Mr. Butthole it is then," I said as he veered off into an alcove of lockers.

He exhaled as he put in his combination. "Kel," he said suddenly, like he wasn't sure he was going to say it until it burst free. "My name's Kel."

"I'm Quinn," I said, realizing the busy hallway had cleared quickly.

"Wait." His head turned toward me as he opened his locker. "You mean your name isn't Idid?"

My arms crossed. "If only."

He came close to smiling again, not one of the tipped or condescending varieties. The real kind.

"What good's your backpack going to do you in there during class?"

He slung a strap over one shoulder, slamming his locker shut. "About the same amount of good it would do me if I had it strapped to my person like you keep yours."

'Then why bring it to school at all?"

He waved at some kids in the hall as we rounded into it. "To blend in."

My eyebrows knitted together. Whatever Kel did in the halls of Riverview High was the opposite of blending in.

As we moved toward the outside doors, my desperation to make an ally in this school took over. "What do you do for lunch?"

"What most people do for lunch," he replied, raising his shoulder. "Eat."

"I was thinking maybe tomorrow, if you don't mind, we could—"

He stopped suddenly. He pivoted to face me, but his eyes stared off somewhere else. "Listen, I've clearly given you the wrong impression," he started, retreating another step. "There are plenty of people to make friends with here." His chin lifted at the crowded courtyard in front of us. "But I'm not one of them."

It was still raining, and as I blinked water away, I did my best to look like I hadn't just been snubbed by the one person I'd had an actual conversation with today.

"Why not?" The words slipped free before I could stop them.

He turned toward the courtyard, picking up the pace. "A-S," he called back before disappearing into the crowd.

It's okay to not be okay. Be sad,
down some ice cream, and embrace the
new life you've found yourself in.

Drowning. That's how I arrived at the apartment.

"Quinn?" His voice came from his bedroom. "There's a pizza in the freezer for you for dinner tonight."

I sloshed inside the apartment, leaving a trail of water droplets as I beelined for my room. "Okay, thanks," I muttered.

"Whoa." Nick emerged from his room, freezing in the middle of tucking in his worn flannel shirt when he saw me. "You're soaking wet."

"Result of walking in the rain." I kept going to my room, eager to change into dry clothes and dish about the disaster that was my life with whatever friend I could get on the phone back home.

"How was your first day?" Nick's footsteps followed me.

"Super," I answered.

"Really?" He rubbed at the back of his head.

"It went exactly how I figured it would." *Worst day ever.*

"That's a relief," he said as I ducked behind the curtains of my room. "I know Riverview High's a lot different from the school you came from, and some of those kids can be pretty intimidating."

Yeah, I met the captain of the intimidating crew.

"It's not too different," I lied, kicking off my Birkenstocks to hopefully dry by next month.

"I think the secret is getting in with the right group of people."

"As opposed to what? The wrong group?" I couldn't help the sting of resentment that hit me whenever Nick tried his hand at parenting.

"Well, it wouldn't be hard to do with that bunch. There are a lot of tough characters at that school. Dead-end kids doing dead-end things."

"I wouldn't want to put myself in that kind of situation, would I?"

Whether he picked up on the sarcasm in my voice or not, he didn't give away. Instead, his footsteps moved through the room, heavy-sounding. "My shift starts soon," he said, opening the door. "I'll be home around three. Make sure and keep the door locked behind me."

Once I heard the dead bolt turn over, I changed from the rest of my wet clothes. They hit the floor with a loud *thwack*, reminding me to grab my raincoat from my still-packed duffel and set it by my backpack, so I wouldn't forget it tomorrow.

Now changed into comfy sweats and an old summer-camp tee, I grabbed my phone to shoot a quick text to Megan. She was one of my besties in Leavenworth, thanks to growing up next to each other the first few years of our lives. Then I sent another text to Raven and Colby for good measure.

I was desperate to talk to one, any, of my friends, but I was on fumes when it came to my data plan for the month. As it was, I wasn't sure the texts would go through.

I'd just hit send on Colby's when Megan got back to me.

What r u thinking texting me after your first day at new school?!?! CALL ME!!!

Warmth spread through me reading her message. Friend. A being on this planet who liked my company instead of avoiding it like I was a social plague.

Calling now, I typed, and right as I hit send, I got the notification that I'd hit my data limit for the month. There were still seven days left in the billing cycle.

My shoulders slumped, regretting the day I'd suggested to Mom we put ourselves on a set plan that wouldn't allow data overages. At the time, medical bills had been steep and penny-pinching was the priority

Now it felt like the kiss of death.

My cell phone was useless. I felt downright primitive.

When I got to school in the morning, I'd have to be sure to fire off a quick email to Megan letting her know about my cell phone woes. Today might have been a disaster, but tomorrow was another day. The worst was behind me. I'd already accepted my curtained bedroom and survived the first day at a new high school—nothing could top that.

Snooping through every cupboard and drawer to see if

there was anything that didn't contain a hundred preserva-tives, I gave up when I found an expired can of Spam with a crust of dust on it. Going for the junk drawer, I grabbed some paper and a pen. I tore off a sheet, scribbled down a quick note, and stuck it to the fridge.

Do you mind if I take over grocery shopping duty? I read. Concise without being too rude or overly polite. Exactly the tone I wanted to set when it came to Nick: giving him no hope that I was game for a father-daughter reunion.

Before leaving the kitchen, I checked the pizza he'd men-tioned, surprised to find it not coated in ice. It looked like he'd picked it up recently . . . right along with twenty Hun-gry Man frozen dinners.

Making my way through the living room, I took my time checking out the apartment for the first time since arriv-ing. With Nick gone, I felt more comfortable letting myself explore the nooks and crannies I'd ignored so far. All the furniture was a couple of decades old, the lampshades in desperate need of a good dusting. Nothing matched, from the drab green sofa to the rose La-Z-Boy to the plywood tele-vision stand.

There's something to be said for simplicity, but this veered more into the survival spectrum. The floor creaked as I roamed the room, completing my walk-through quickly since there was no fluff to stop and inspect. The walls were bare of pictures, the flat surfaces were empty of any kind of decor or books, and there was nothing personal about the space other than the trail of worn-down carpet that ran from Nick's room to the front door.

My feet took me to Nick's bedroom. His door was half

closed. Reaching inside, I flipped on the light switch. I had no expectations for what I'd find. A bed, a dresser, and a brass lamp resting on one of those plastic storage containers like I had in my room came into view. It was tidy, but not exactly clean, same as the rest of the apartment. Everything was put away, but I wasn't sure a mirror had been cleaned or a surface dusted since Nick moved in however many years ago.

For all the perks the bachelor life supposedly had from the outside, it seemed pretty sucky from the inside.

I was about to turn the light off when something caught my attention tucked behind the stack of laundry folded on the dresser. It was a picture frame, but the photo inside was obscured by the clothes, so I had to take a few steps closer.

My body froze the moment I saw it. The photo was of my mom holding me. I couldn't have been older than two, and we were both laughing, like whatever Nick had said as he took the picture had been funny. Probably one of those lame jokes he used to come home from work every day and tell me. Back then, they'd been funny. Now they just made me sad.

Leaving his room, I shut off the lights and closed the door behind me. All the way.

It was Friday, and I was the only one who wasn't celebrating the countdown to two days of impending freedom at Riverview High.

My second day had been a carbon copy of my first. One of the first to arrive, going through security, sitting at my own table of one, milling between classes feeling more specter than human. The handful of times I'd gone out of my way to say hi or compliment the person sitting beside me was met with disregard, or the occasional side-eye paired with an expression that read *Who the hell are you?*

When it came time for chem, I dropped onto the same stool I'd taken yesterday, nervously checking the entrance waiting for Kel to come in even though the bell had already rung. I hadn't seen him at all today—not that I'd been looking for him particularly.

Mr. Johnson was leaning into the whiteboard up front, taking attendance. When he got to the empty seat beside me, he blinked at me. "What did you do to scare away the supposedly unscareable Mr. Remington, Miss Winters?"

He was just joking, getting right back to taking attendance, but heat rushed behind my cheeks. Mr. Johnson acknowledged my existence, but it wasn't exactly the kind of attention I was going for. Thinking of what had happened yesterday with Kel—thinking of him at all—came with an unwelcome cascade of emotions.

"Today we'll be doing a lab, Intrepid Minds, so buddy up and I'll hand out the details." Mr. Johnson wove through the room, distributing lab worksheets. When he got to me, I was the only person not paired up.

"Team of one today, Miss Winters?" He smiled.

"Team of one every day," I replied, feeling like a trend was emerging.

*I'd rather trust and be wrong
than doubt and be right.*

"Something sure smells good, Quinn Bee," Nick said as he came into the apartment Sunday night.

My shoulders went rigid. Quinn Bee had been my childhood nickname, born from a streak of toddler sassiness. I used to "rule the hive," he claimed. But I wasn't a toddler anymore, and I didn't rule at anything these days.

"Whatcha making?" he asked, taking a seat on the old couch and untying his work boots.

"Enchiladas," I replied, checking the oven to distract myself.

"Your mom's recipe?" His voice went up a note.

Mom made the best enchiladas around. It was a well-known fact in Leavenworth. Both locals and tourists regularly visited the restaurant she was a chef at because she could not make a bad meal.

"Just the recipe on the back of the enchilada-sauce can." I chucked the can into the recycle bin, wondering why I'd decided to make enchiladas at all when mine would never compare to Mom's anyway.

"Well, I'm sure they'll be just as good," he replied, stuffing his boots beside the sofa and wiggling his toes. "Thanks again for offering to pick up on grocery and meal detail. I don't mind doing it—"

"I'm happy to," I interrupted, checking the oven again before deciding the cheese had reached the ideal melty-meets-bubbling stage.

"Happy?" The doubt in Nick's voice was palpable.

"Content," I settled on as I grabbed the new oven mitt I'd picked up.

Nick cleared his throat. "Do you need any help in there?"

"Nope. Dinner's ready." I pulled the tray of enchiladas from the oven and carried them to the card table. I'd stacked a couple of towels to set the plates on so as not to burn right through.

"What do you want to drink?" Nick roamed into the kitchen, seeming as uncertain as I did. It was the first time we'd actually sat down to a meal together, and it appeared we both needed instructions for how to go about it.

"Water," I replied, busying myself with mixing the salad that was sufficiently mixed. "Thanks."

"Yeah, I think I'll have the same." Nick opened the fridge first, peering inside for a minute before realizing cups were in the cupboard and water was in the faucet.

This was already so awkward and we hadn't even sat down to eat yet. I began dishing the enchiladas, sliding an extra one onto his plate in front of the larger chair of the two at the table. Nick and I had settled into something of a pattern since I'd moved in—a pattern of avoiding one another. Not that it was overly intentional or born from malice, but I went to school during the days, and he was nearly on his way to work when I got back. Saturday and today he'd been gone doing "errands," but I couldn't imagine what type of errands a guy like Nick did. They weren't grocery-shopping or home-improvement ones, that was for sure.

"Oh, did you see my answer to your leadership shirt question?" He pointed to the fridge, where we'd developed a system of communication that worked for two people who lived in the same space but rarely occupied it at the same time. If one of us had a question, we'd write it down on the piece of paper I'd stuck to the fridge when I'd requested meal duty. Then a response would magically appear.

It was about as odd and impersonal as it got, but that suited me just fine. From the lack of objection from Nick, I assumed he felt the same.

"Yeah, thanks." I moved on to dishing the salad next, accidentally dropping half a scoop on the table instead of my plate. "I guess the teacher wants everyone in leadership class to wear their Riverview High Pride shirts on Fridays in hopes of boosting school spirit or something." I wiped the spilled salad off the table onto my hand. "Which, if you're going to 'strongly encourage' your students to wear some school shirt every week, it seems like you'd at least *provide* the shirts instead of having us pay for them."

"Ten dollars doesn't seem like much to ask for a nice T-shirt."

"It's the principle. The teacher's pretty much telling us we have to wear them, and then on top of that expecting us to foot the bill." I brushed the salad from my hands into the garbage, surprised I was having a conversation with Nick. Voluntarily. It had to do with being desperate for human interaction, since I had yet to make a new friend, but I would have thought it would take months of solitary confinement before I'd be willing to have a conversation with the guy who bailed on my mom and me.

Apparently, I was far weaker than I thought.

The comforting revelations just kept rolling in.

"I put a can on top of the fridge—call it a petty cash stash." Nick's gaze moved to an old coffee can. "That way if any school things come up or you need a few bucks to get ice cream with your friends, you'll be covered. No need to ask me or anything. I'll just make sure to keep a bit in it all the time for that kind of stuff." He settled into his chair after standing beside it for a moment, as perplexed by this whole sit-down meal as I was. "Okay?"

My eyes roamed everywhere but across the table as I settled into the chair behind my plate. "Okay," I said. "Thanks."

I wasn't expecting it to be so easy. Or his generosity to be so proactive.

After that, there was an uncomfortable silence.

Nick took a long drink of his water, shifting in his chair. "Why don't they play poker in the jungle?"

"What?" My face twisted with confusion.

There was a glint in his eyes, half a smile in place. He

circled his fork and repeated, "Why don't they play poker in the jungle?"

He was trying to tell a joke, I realized. But I didn't want to hear a joke.

I wanted my mom back, along with the entirety of my old life.

When I stayed quiet, continuing to pick my enchilada apart, he leaned forward. "Because there's too many cheetahs," he said with such enthusiasm, it was as if he'd made the joke up on his own.

I rubbed at my eye like something was in it, when really I was just trying to hold off the tears. "There aren't any cheetahs in the jungle. They live in the savannah."

The moment I saw his face, I wanted to take back what I'd said. But I couldn't. Mom had always taught me to think twice about the words I spoke because I had only one chance to say them. While kids were chanting the "sticks and stones" jingle, Mom was preaching about how words were the hardest-hitting objects we could throw at a person. The look on Nick's face was a reminder of that lesson.

He was trying. A little. I gave him credit for that, but it didn't come close to making up for leaving us the way he had. A "petty cash" box and a room constructed of cotton and a corny joke didn't erase a decade of abandonment.

Nick worked on his dinner, eating it without really seeming to taste it. "This is damn good." The corners of his eyes creased when he caught himself. "I mean darn. Might not be your mom's recipe, but it's just as delicious."

"Thanks," I muttered, knowing nothing could ever be as good as Mom's anything, enchiladas included.

Nick set his fork down. "Hey, I noticed earlier that your phone doesn't seem to be working." He shifted in his chair, almost like he was anticipating me going off on him for snooping around my personal effects.

"Um, yeah. I'm out of data for the month. But it's only for a few more days."

He was quiet for a minute. The quiet stretched on awkwardly. "How about this? What if I put my bank account on your cell phone plan, and we upped your data?" He took a quick sip of his water, gauging my reaction across the table. "With me not having a landline, I don't like the idea of you not being able to make calls or check in, especially while I'm working nights."

Something lodged in my throat, making it hard to reply. I reached for my water.

"It's important you're able to make phone calls, in the event of an emergency or something"—his face was lined, focused—"and with you taking over the grocery shopping and meal making responsibilities, I really must insist—"

"That would be great." I set my water glass down, realizing this was the first time I'd looked him straight in the eyes. "Thank you."

Your fear is big.
But your courage is bigger.

Fridays might have been a party, but Mondays were more like a funeral. I'd know.

Half of first period trudged in tardy or not at all; second wasn't much better. By third, most everyone was accounted for, but that might have mostly had to do with the subject: leadership. It wouldn't look great if the supposed leaders of the school were skipping classes like the rest of Riverview High.

When the bell rang at the end of third, I stalled, waiting for the rest of the room to clear before I did. Mrs. Guthrie caught me as I was still packing up.

"Quinn," she called, approaching with a paper in her hand. "I didn't have a chance to go over this with you last week, but a requirement of leadership is to fulfill forty hours of community service."

I took the sheet from her. "My old school had that too. No problem."

"This is a list of organizations and projects you can apply those hours to," she said. "Take a look and let me know tomorrow which option you want to go with—that's fine. I just didn't want to waste any more time as we're already a month into the new semester. Forty hours is a lot."

As I scanned the worksheet, I noticed the usual volunteer opportunities—animal shelters, litter clean-up, soup kitchens, the typical do-gooder fare; but I needed something that would work for the carless and the still slightly intimidated by Seattle's public transportation alternatives. In Leavenworth, I could bike to pretty much everywhere I needed or wanted to go.

The last option caught my attention. "After-school tutoring," I announced, relieved when I saw the location listed as Riverview High's library. "I'll do that for my forty hours."

Mrs. Guthrie propped her reading glasses on top of her head. "Are you sure?" From her tone, I felt like she was almost trying to talk me out of it. Like I'd picked the booby prize and she was giving me a chance to change my mind.

I gave it another thought. "Yeah, I'm sure. I did some tutoring at my old school, and I enjoyed it."

"Okay then," she said, flipping open a folder and jotting something down. "I'll talk to Mrs. Peterson, the head of the tutoring program, to match you up. I'll get you a name in a few days."

"Sounds great. Thanks."

"Hey, Quinn?" she called as I turned to leave.

"Yeah?"

Mrs. Guthrie closed her folder. "How's everything going? I know it's not easy starting late in a school this size. New students have a way of disappearing in the masses sometimes."

I practiced my smile before glancing at her. "It's going all right."

"Gotten to know some of the students here?"

My smile held. "Getting there."

"You just gotta find your tribe, you know?"

I angled toward the room. "Find my tribe?"

Mrs. Guthrie waved at the classroom. "You know, your people. The ones who get you. The fools who will drive the getaway van." She winked as she said it. "Kidding about the last part."

"What if I don't know what my tribe is?"

She came around her desk, taking a seat on the edge of it. "Who did you hang with at your last school? Who were your friends?"

"Everyone," I replied.

"Everyone?"

"It was a small school. Like thirty kids in my class small. We'd all been going to school with each other since kindergarten."

Mrs. Guthrie was quiet a moment. Then she smiled. "Well, it may take some time, but trust me, they're out there. Your tribe will find you." Waving at me, she went back behind her desk to dig into her lunch.

Lunch.

It was my break for that as well, but it had easily become my least favorite time of the day. I hated feeling like I was hiding from Riverview High. And I hated eating alone and feeling alone and being alone. I hated most, though, feeling like a coward.

By the time I made it to the cafeteria entrance, I was barely moving forward at all. From the outside, it seemed like everyone belonged at some table, to some "tribe." Everyone had a place at Riverview High except me.

I found myself wishing I could have been like my mom, who would've marched in there and plopped down at the most interesting-appearing table and twenty minutes later won over a posse of new besties. She was a natural when it came to making friends; she'd radiated a natural exuberance that people were drawn to. My eyes began to well at the thought of my mom's moxie. Out of desperation, I turned to flee the cafeteria, but the first step I took, I crashed into something. Or someone.

Ouifph was the sound I made mid-impact.

"Shit, sorry," a familiar voice said as a large pair of hands kept me from falling. He realized who he'd run into before I did. "Quinn. Hey." Kel's jaw worked, his hands releasing me. "Sorry about that."

Kel. I hadn't seen him in days. Why did the first time I did have to be when I was rushing to the girls' bathroom to have a meltdown?

"Pretty sure that was my fault. So I should be the one

saying sorry." I bit at my lip, checking my arms to make sure his hands weren't there any longer. They weren't, but I could still feel them.

When I went to dodge around him, he leapt in front of me. His face was drawn up, his eyes searching. When he stayed quiet, I moved around him again. This time he let me go.

I was halfway down the hall before he called my name. "Are you okay?"

My throat tightened hearing the tone of his voice. Concern. I could just detect it. Why him? Why did it always have to be him?

"We're not friends. Remember, Kel?" I looked away and kept moving. "You don't have to pretend like you actually care."

I made it to sixth period. At least the beginning of it. It was no longer a countdown in days but in classes. How many classes did I have to endure before I'd be out of here? The idea of emancipation was becoming more tempting. Anything was better than spending the next two-plus years stuck in this place.

Pulling my notebook from my bag, I noticed a figure lumber into class a minute after the bell had sounded.

"Mr. Remington. How nice of you to grace us with your presence, albeit tardy. I'm relieved you remembered you had a class sixth period." Mr. Johnson gave his best stern face, but it fell way flat.

Kel replied with a half-assed salute. I found myself holding my breath as he approached my lab table. After our run-in in the hallway, I wasn't sure whether I was hoping he'd sit down or keep going.

He ambled past me, finally choosing an empty stool at a table in the opposite corner of the classroom.

Mr. Johnson dove into his lecture, but I found myself unable to pay attention. The air in the room had changed, and I knew it didn't have to do with the new unit on intermolecular forces. It was him. *Kel.*

I found myself glancing around the room to see if anyone else was under the same impression that the atmosphere had become charged with something more potent than electricity. Bored faces, a few slyly checking phones tucked in their laps, the rest pretending to be paying attention.

Nope, it was just me.

Which was another reason I needed to get away from this place.

The person who had made it insanely clear that he didn't want to have any sort of association with me was the one I felt some strange feeling for whenever he was around. The universe was laughing at me, I swear.

"Miss Winters? Are you with us?" Mr. Johnson's voice cut through my haze.

"Yeah, I am," I replied, sitting up and adjusting my pencil over my notebook like I'd been taking notes.

"Then can you answer the question I directed your way two times now?" Mr. Johnson circled his hand, waiting.

My cheeks burned. I had no memory of one thing he'd said in his lesson today, and I definitely didn't have a memory of the question he'd asked me. Twice.

"I'm sorry." I tucked my hair behind my ear. "I don't know the answer."

A snicker echoed through the class.

Something caught my attention as I shifted on my stool. Someone was holding a sheet of paper with big black letters written on it.

HOW WAS YOUR WEEKEND?

My forehead lined at Kel. His eyes lifted as he pointed a black marker at Mr. Johnson before aiming it at the question he'd scratched down on the paper.

"Good." It spilled from my mouth. "My weekend was good. Thanks," I finished, wishing the floor could open up and swallow me whole this very second.

"Glad to hear it, Miss Winters. Finally." Mr. Johnson shot me a smile as he moved on to the next student.

Across the room, I could feel his stare. Why had Kel helped me? Why did he care?

When I finally worked up the courage to return that stare, I found him focusing on the front of the room, where Mr. Johnson was scribbling down something on the whiteboard. I watched him for a few seconds, waiting.

Kel Remington never looked my way again.

You don't get to choose your family,
but you get to choose your friends.
Choose wisely.

"Okay, seriously, though, how is it? Better or worse than you thought it would be?"

On the other end of the line, Megan waited while I decided which answer to give her: the truth or what I wished was the truth.

"Worse."

I decided to go with the truth.

"Ugh. Seriously?" It sounded like she was flopping down on her bed. "You had already prepared yourself for it being the worst thing imaginable. How can it be worse than that?"

I pinched at my bedroom "walls." "You do recall I mentioned that my room is made of curtains, right?"

"Yeah," she said, sighing with me. "How's the new school?"

"It's a new school." Bouncing off my bed, I headed for the kitchen in search of a snack.

"Made any friends?"

"Not exactly," I said in the cheeriest voice I could muster.

"Seriously? How is that possible?" Meg huffed. "You're, like, the nicest person in the world."

"I don't know. Exceptionally bad luck?" As I pulled the fridge open to scavenge whatever was left, I noticed a new note scratched down in Nick's choppy handwriting.

What do you get from a pampered cow?

The answer was written at the very bottom of the note sheet in smaller letters:

Spoiled milk.

"Why are you laughing?" Meg asked.

I didn't realize I was until she called me on it. "It's nothing. Just some dumb joke Nick wrote on the fridge."

"Tell me. I need a good joke after learning one of my besties is miserable and all I can do is provide emotional support over the phone."

"Trust me, I'll take emotional support in whatever form you want to send it. Even if it's just in positive vibes sent via brain waves."

"Noted," she said. "Now tell me the joke."

"It's not funny."

"Then why did you laugh?"

"Because it was so not funny it was funny." I scooted

milk and pickles around until I found the last container of yogurt tucked into the back.

"Fine. Be that way." She tried on her best annoyed voice, but it needed some work. "But really, though. You haven't made any friends?"

After ripping the foil seal from the yogurt, I gave it a lick and snagged a spoon from the drawer. "No friends. Yet. I don't think people are trying to be mean or intentionally ignoring me, but everyone already has their group of friends and doesn't seem to be in the market for making any more."

"There's not even a random loner you could link up with?"

"Do you know the definition of loner?" I replied.

"Wait, are *you* becoming a loner?"

"Loners choose their solitude. Mine was chosen for me. I think that makes me more pitiful." My nose wrinkled as I sat at the table to eat my yogurt. With the new cell phone plan, I'd gotten to talk to my friends back home every night, which made my disaster of a life in Renton seem less overwhelming. It was still a mess, but at least I had people to laugh about it with. Plus life with Nick was getting easier, and he didn't give me a hard time about drinking coffee like Mom had.

"Listen, I've got a paper to finish tonight, so I should probably let you go. Thanks for listening to me whine. Again."

"That's what friends are for." The chip bag Meg had been snacking on in the background stopped rustling. "Hey, Quinn?" She paused a moment, giving me a chance to brace for what I knew she was about to bring up. "How are you doing? How are you *really* doing?"

Setting my spoon down, I pushed my yogurt aside. Appetite gone. "I'm fine."

52

"Fine is like the definition of not fine—you know that, right?"

"Megan, I'm good. I swear." I got up to head to my room. Moving somehow made the heavy stuff easier to digest.

"Your mom just died. I know you're not fine or good or whatever you're going to tell me next."

I rubbed at my forehead as I paced. "I'm not in the mood to talk about it all right now, okay? I know you care, and thank you for that, but I just can't go there."

Meg didn't sigh or protest on the other end like I half expected. Instead she let a minute of quiet pass; then the chip bag went back to rustling. "You need to be here next month for sure. It's Raven's birthday, I'm hosting, and you cannot miss it. Music, dancing, enough pizza to put this whole city into a food coma. You *have* to come."

Birthday parties. People who liked me. Pizza from the local place in town I'd probably eaten at a thousand times. Home. "I don't know how I'll get there. Bus tickets are expensive, and I'm not going to ask Nick to drive me."

"Why not? He's your father. It's his parental duty to be inconvenienced by his child. Especially inconvenienced when that child is a teenage girl and one he skipped out on for a solid decade."

"Thanks for the recap," I muttered.

"You know I'm right."

The thought of asking Nick to drive me to Leavenworth was about as appealing as asking him to join me on a mission to Mars. The awkward silence would drag on forever in either scenario.

"I'll think about it," I said.

"You'll go for it," Meg said in her voice that suggested it

53

was all settled. "I'll let everyone know we'll get to see you in a few weeks. It'll fly by."

I didn't want to tell her I hadn't been in Renton for a week and it had already felt like an eternity.

I survived another week at Riverview High. Still as friendless as the day I started, I'd adopted the attitude of embracing my party-of-one plight. *It is what it is.* Another Mom-ism I was taking to heart. Plus knowing I had an exit strategy made putting up with the day-to-day easier. Emancipation. The light at the end of the tunnel made all the difference.

I'd spent a couple of hours after class all week in the library collecting the paperwork. Emancipating was just the proverbial tip of the iceberg—figuring out how to live on my own was the real hurdle. Growing up with a person like my mom had made me pretty independent, but I was fifteen. What landlord would take me seriously? And I'd still have to find a job to pay rent.

The library was my destination after school today too, but not to research emancipation. It was my first volunteer tutoring session. Mrs. Guthrie didn't have a name for me yet but told me to show up after school and someone would be waiting. She assured me the tutoring committee was setting it up.

As expected, the library was dead. Toward the opposite end near the study tables, I could see one lone student sprawled in a chair with his back to me.

A guy. I don't know why I'd assumed I'd be paired with a girl, but before the surprise of realizing I'd be spending forty hours with some random dude wore off, I froze in place.

Oversized white tee, shoulders you could balance a Prius on, and that messy mop of dark hair.

Twisting in his chair, when he saw me standing there with god only knows what kind of look on my face, he grinned. "I suppose I should have known it would be you," he said, scooting his chair away from the table a little. "Smart girl, dumb boy." His finger pointed from me to him.

"You're the one I'm supposed to be tutoring?" I managed to get out once I could finally form words.

"Unless there's another kid in your leadership class who picked forty hours of tutoring some dumb shit, then yeah, you got stuck with me." His shoulder lifted. "Sorry."

My eyes narrowed as I contemplated the universe's twisted sense of humor. "What subject do you need help with?" I threw myself together as much as I could and continued toward his table.

He watched me come closer. "All of them."

"Seriously?"

"You want to check my grades?"

When I stopped beside the chair he'd kicked out for me, I had to go through a mental checklist of what to do next. Take off bag. Sit down. Blink. Breathe.

This boy was officially making me unbalanced.

"What subject do you want to begin with, then?" I asked.

"You pick. Coach is going to bench me unless I get all my grades up. Doesn't matter if we start with math or English."

I shuffled through the books in my bag, pulling one free. "Fine. Chemistry it is."

Kel pressed into the table, his dark eyes finding mine. "One of my favorite subjects."

I flipped open the chapter we were working on, biting my tongue to keep from firing something back. He was messing with me again, and I didn't like being a magnet for his teasing. "It helps if you actually open a book and have a piece of paper in front of you. A writing implement also tends to be useful."

Kel rubbed at his mouth to hide his smile as he reached for his backpack.

"Oh, you actually have a pencil in that thing?"

"You actually believe in that school pride shit you're wearing?" Kel pointed at my shirt, the one all of us leadership students were supposed to wear on Fridays. "Riverview Tigers: Where everyone's a part of the team."

I rolled my eyes at his sarcastic tone. "Of course I do," I answered, blinking. "Everyone's a part of the team. Except for me."

That uneven smile of his appeared again. "Try you *and* me."

"Please. You are like the unofficial captain of the entire team. Nice try."

"Oh yeah? When's the last time you've seen me rolling down the halls with a posse? Or clustered up with a bunch of kids in class?" One dark brow lifted at me. "I'm a team of one. Just like you, Idid."

My arms dropped at my sides. "*Whatever.* You could walk up to any table at lunch and take a seat, and it would be fine."

At that, Kel laughed and then clasped his hands in front of him on the table. "Since you clearly haven't figured it out yet, I'm going to let you in on a little secret. High school, this place?" His quiet words were warm against my cheek. "None of this is real. It's an act. All of it."

I cleared my throat. "An act?"

"High school is a stage, and every one of us students is playing a role." Kel finally reclined in his chair. "So if you don't like the role you're playing, pick a different one."

My eyebrows pulled together. "I'm not playing a role. I'm being myself."

Kel grunted. "You're acting right now. Pretending like having to sit across from me and attempt to teach my stupid ass something for forty hours is no big deal. You play a role walking down these halls every day, pretending like you don't care that you're the new kid when it's really damn obvious you do."

My gaze had shifted to the textbook as I thumbed through it, welcoming any excuse to be distracted. "You don't know me." My words were more cutting than I'd intended, not that they made Kel flinch. He moved in closer instead, like sharp things attracted instead of scared him.

"I know. But I recognize an act when I see one." He was waiting for me to make eye contact, but he could wait forever for all I cared. I wasn't looking him in the eyes. He'd already seen enough inside them. "Don't like the role, pick a different one. Easy as that."

My pencil was rapping against my chemistry book.

"You really believe that? Everyone's just playing some big role?"

He scribbled the date down on the piece of paper. "The bigger the act, the bigger the fake."

My head tipped as I watched him slide the pencil behind

his ear, the dawn of a smirk settling on his face where his lower lip had been split open recently. Sitting there like he owned the place. "What about you? What role are you playing?"

Kel motioned at himself. "I'm not playing a role."

I pointed my pencil straight at him, not blinking. Maybe he could see through me, but I could see through some of him, too. "Translation: you're playing the biggest role of all."

A corner of his mouth pulled up, his posture relaxing some. "You're a quick study. I guess that's why you're on that side of the tutoring table and I'm over here, barely able to write my name without fucking up." He gave a small wince. "Sorry. Language."

I waved it off, annoyed that he assumed I'd be offended, and reminded myself why we were here in the first place. "If you insist on playing a role, how about you pretend to be an obedient student for a while? Let's do a quick review of what we went over in class this week. Sound good?"

"Lead the way, Teach."

"First lesson." I paused for dramatic effect. "I don't like nicknames. So Idid, Teach, and whatever other gems you might devise in the future, just keep them to yourself."

"Whatever you say." He seemed to catch himself just in time. "*Quinn*."

When I started to chuckle, so did Kel. His laugh was about as hesitant and impaired sounding as mine.

"So, okay. Chemistry." My pencil thumped the chapter review page for the section we'd just finished in class. "There's a practice quiz on page forty-seven. Start there, and I'll be able to see what you need the most help with before the test next week."

"Besides everything," he muttered as he flipped to the same page I was on and read the first problem.

It took him almost five minutes to finish question one, and another twenty to work out the next four. He'd gotten all of them wrong except for the second problem, which frankly may have just been a lucky guess, so I stopped him.

"Maybe we should back up a bit. Why don't we start at the beginning of the chapter and work our way through it a little at a time? It would be a good review for me, too."

"Smell that?" Kel sniffed at the air. "It's the scent of pants on fire."

"Sense that?" I argued back, giving his arm a soft shove. "It's the feeling of not amused."

The sound of something being dropped at the front of the library got our attention. I saw the giant trash can on wheels first; then I started when I saw who was standing behind it. I didn't know what to do, wave at him or pretend I hadn't seen him.

Nick made the decision for me.

"What is this, Quinn?"

Kel scanned between Nick and me.

"Fulfilling my forty hours of community service for leadership." I tapped my book with my pencil, expecting Nick to finish whatever he was doing and keep going.

He stayed planted in place, his focus moving to Kel. His arms crossed. "How did you wind up with him?" Tone made all the difference in the world. Nick's suggested Kel was the last person on the planet anyone should want sitting across a table from them.

"Unluck of the draw," Kel broke in before I could reply.

Nick didn't find any humor in Kel's answer. "How long is this tutoring supposed to go tonight?"

My grip on my pencil tightened. Nick hadn't earned the right to tell me who I should and shouldn't spend time with. "I don't know. Another hour or so."

"And after that, you're heading home. Alone." He moved a bit farther into the library, narrowed eyes still fixed on Kel like he was a rabid animal about to pounce.

"Yeah," I answered, my tone hopefully relaying that he could get back to his own life and leave mine alone. Like he'd made a priority of it for a decade. Where had the mellow, couldn't-care-less Nick gone?

"Okay. I'll be close by. If you need me." He didn't stop glaring at Kel until he disappeared into the hall.

That was just awesome. As if my status at Riverview High wasn't already caked with mud, now I had Terminator Dad, the night custodian, to add to the dirt on the new girl.

"Sorry about that," I said, hoping my cheeks weren't too flushed from embarrassment. "He's not usually so 'invested.'"

"Your dad?" Kel's voice was normal. He didn't sound the least bit pissed at Nick's behavior.

"In the loosest sense of the word."

"What about your mom?"

I focused on keeping my voice even. "She's dead."

Kel was quiet for a moment. "Is that why you moved?"

"Yeah," I said, drawing scribbles into the corner of my paper. "She died last month and decided to leave me in the hands of him instead of any one of the dozens of other people back home."

"But he's your dad."

The lead of my pencil broke. "He's barely my dad. He ditched us when I was five, and I never heard a word from him until now."

Kel handed me his pencil so I could keep scribbling. "That's cold."

I huffed. "More like frigid."

"Then why would your mom leave you with him?"

The unanswerable question came up again. "Your guess is as good as mine. What about you? What's your family like?"

Kel's expression flattened for an instant before he recovered. Checking the clock, he stood up and began packing his bag. "It's a Friday. You've got better things to do than try to teach my sorry ass."

"It hasn't even been an hour," I said, checking the time. At this rate I'd have to meet up with him forty plus times to get my hours completed. I wasn't sure I could survive another if our conversations continued to follow the same pattern.

"Nah, it's been two." He threw his bag over his shoulder, waiting for me.

"Kel, no, it hasn't."

"Listen, I know you don't want to be here with me, and it would take a hell of a lot more than forty hours to get my grades up. I'll just mark down a few hours every week that we spent together, and you can turn that in at the end of the semester."

My head shook as I stuffed my things into my bag. "That's lying."

"Lying?" He gave me an amused smirk. "Coming from Miss Pants on Fire?"

When I handed him his pencil, he slipped it into his back pocket but didn't take off.

"What are you waiting for?" I finally asked.

"You."

Shouldering my bag, I headed toward the door. Kel fell in beside me.

"I'm a good tutor, you know. If we spend forty hours together actually doing schoolwork, your grades will go up."

"I'm a worse student."

I checked the hallway before leaving in case Nick was lying in wait.

"Why did you agree to tutoring in the first place, then, if you had no intentions of actually following through with it?" I asked, keeping my voice quiet and my pace quick. Nick was nowhere in sight and I wanted to keep it that way.

"I thought it maybe could help, but now I'm pretty sure nothing but a brain transplant will make a difference."

"Aren't you going to get benched if you don't get your GPA up?" I asked, remembering what he'd said earlier.

Kel sighed. "Yeah. Probably."

I checked the next hall to make sure it was clear. "What sport do you play? Besides Fight Club," I asked, noting his split-open, swollen lip.

"Baseball." The way he said it was like the way a parent said their child's name. Like it was priceless.

"Baseball, really?" My forehead pulled together. "I took you more as the full-contact-sport type."

"Sorry to surprise you," he said.

When we reached the doors, Kel moved in front of me to shove them open for me. The strange boy had manners. Some. "You surprise me a lot actually. Baseball, huh? Now I really have to tutor you. I like baseball."

"Sure ya do," he said, falling in beside me again as we started for the quiet parking lot. There were just a few cars left. When I stopped at the crosswalk, he paused with me.

"Oh-kay, I'll see you later, I guess," I said.

As I turned to head toward the street, Kel asked, "Don't you drive to school?" His arm swung into the parking lot.

"I'm fifteen."

Kel jogged to catch up to me. "Is that your way of saying you don't drive, then? Because I was ten the first time I climbed behind a wheel."

"Have a bubble-gum emergency or something?"

"Or something." His feet crunched as they moved across the gravel-littered sidewalk. Mine barely registered.

"Can't answer like that and not expect a follow-up question."

Kel kind of glared into the looming darkness, like he was the one to be scared of. "Mom needed to get to the emergency room, and she wasn't in any condition to get there herself."

When I turned down the next block past the high school, Kel stayed with me. "What happened?" I asked hesitantly.

"She broke her wrist." He paused, his jaw moving. "And, well, she shouldn't have been behind the wheel even if she hadn't."

"What about your dad? Couldn't he have taken her?"

Kel's jaw moved.

"He's not in the picture?" I asked gently.

"He's not anything." Kel rubbed at one of the scars slicing through his dark brow. "He's not even worth the air it takes to curse his name."

He continued before I could get another word in. "So we're headed this way, then?"

I wanted to know more, but I knew a gridlock when I saw one. Kel wasn't saying anything else. "Yeah—do you live this way too?" I asked, since he was still right beside me.

"Nope."

"Do you drive to school?"

His hands wrapped around the straps of his backpack. "Nope."

"Then what are you doing?"

"Walking."

"Why are you walking this direction?" I gave him the exact tone he'd used on me.

"There's this convenience store up ahead. Makes the best slushies you'll find anywhere."

"Really?"

Kel grumbled. "No, not really." His hand moved between him and me before motioning at the darkening streets. "It's late, dark, and I'm pretty sure the guy is supposed to walk the girl home to make sure she gets there safe and sound."

He glanced over at me the same way I was peering at him. With curiosity.

For the next few blocks, we strolled in silence. Kel Remington was walking me home.

"So, do Fridays after school work for you, then?" I asked when the apartment building came into view.

"At least until baseball practice starts."

"Great, let's plan to meet in the library at the same time until then. Once baseball begins, we can figure out a different schedule."

Kel eyed the guy moving down the sidewalk toward us, moving to my other side before the man passed by. "I thought we decided tutoring was a pointless venture."

"No. *You* decided that. I decided to prove you wrong." I paused when we were in front of the apartment building.

Kel inspected it, his gaze roaming from top to bottom. I shifted, uncomfortable. Not because I was embarrassed by it, but because it felt personal—intimate—sharing it with him.

"Sure you're not just looking for an excuse to hang around me?"

I feigned shock. "Am I that transparent?"

Kel unlatched the cyclone gate, pushing it open for me. "You, Miss Winters, are the least transparent person out there."

"You're one to talk." I lightly nudged the side of his backpack as I passed through the gate. "And you're not nearly as dumb as you try to make people think you are. I was there when you rattled off periodic table elements like it was second nature."

"I knew arsenic. *One* element," he said, hanging his arms over the fence gate. "And I could maybe get a couple others right on a good day."

"You're not stupid, Kel."

"I sure as hell ain't smart, either." He snorted, studying the distance between us. "Want me to walk you inside?"

"I can manage the last few yards by myself. Thanks,

though." I stopped when I realized something. "Now you're going home by yourself in the dark." Size and badassery aside, he was still a sixteen-year-old.

He lifted his chin at me as he latched the gate behind me. "I am the dark. Nothing messes with me."

I shot him a doubtful look as I unlocked the main door.

"Hey, Quinn?" he called as I stepped inside. When I turned, I saw a flash of vulnerability in his eyes. "I'm sorry about your mom. I know she was an awesome person."

Swallow. Inhale. Speak.

"How do you know that?" I asked, my voice a few notes high.

He smiled. Perhaps the first real smile I'd seen from him. Then he motioned at me before heading into the night. "Because you are."

Leave the bad boy alone. For real, Quinn, just keep walking. Heartache and break is all you'll have to show for your efforts to love one.

Rising off the bench, I tucked the journal into my stuffed bag and headed back to the apartment. It was almost five and I still had dinner and homework to finish.

When I unlocked the door and stepped inside the apartment, an unusual aroma greeted—*assaulted*—me. A quick survey of the kitchen explained it. Nick was stationed in front of the stove with a metal spatula in hand, holding it like a hammer he was about to pound something with. Smoke billowed from the couple of pans he had on the stovetop. It was a miracle the smoke alarm hadn't gone off yet.

"Everything okay?" I asked, rushing into the kitchen before whatever was inside the pans caught on fire.

"Everything's under control." Nick didn't turn around,

just towered over the stovetop like he was trying to intimidate dinner into cooperating.

Peeking around him, I crinkled my nose when I saw the scene of the crime. The contents were so charred, it was hard to determine what they'd originally started as.

"What are you making?" I turned the burners from max to off before moving toward the kitchen window to open it.

"Dinner." The spatula in Nick's hand rose higher.

"What kind of dinner?" I asked. *Burned Beyond Recognition Casserole?*

"Salmon and wild rice." When the pan containing what I now knew was rice popped, Nick slapped the spatula down onto it. Bits of charred chunks exploded into the air. "I noticed you like eating healthy stuff, and the guy at the store told me this was healthy."

I laughed. "Pretty sure the number of carcinogens you've managed to burn into that meal cancels out all the health benefits." I grabbed the oven mitt before reaching for the smoking black rock of salmon. "But good effort," I added when I noticed his crestfallen expression.

"That may be the first time I've used the stove for anything other than to make eggs."

"In fairness, it takes practice. Going from boiling water to making salmon is a big leap. Next time, give pasta a try." I turned on the faucet and set the pan inside the sink. The water sizzled and spit when it hit the hot pan, the smoke eventually steaming to an end.

"Sorry," he said, his shoulders slumping. "I was just trying to help. Should have known better."

Even though it was a total disaster, I couldn't help feeling a tinge of gratitude that he'd attempted dinner so I could take the night off.

"Lucky for us I ran to the store earlier." I dropped my bag on the counter, starting to unload groceries. "Spaghetti with marinara will be up in fifteen."

When Nick went to grab the handle of the scorched rice, I handed him the pot holder. "I'm happy to drive you to the store next time. I've got a perfectly good truck, you know?" He watched, impressed, as I finished unloading my stash. I'd fit a good three bags' worth of groceries into one school backpack.

"I don't mind walking. I actually kinda like it."

"A girl . . . woman . . ." Nick rubbed at his forehead. "*Female.*" He paused long enough to give me a moment to protest. I was too busy trying not to laugh at his discomfort. "Shouldn't be walking alone this close to dark in this part of town."

"'This part of town'?" I motioned at the open window. "You make it sound like we live in the middle of Skid Row. It's not that bad."

"Still."

"Then why have you lived here so long?"

"It didn't used to feel that way." He checked up and down the street before closing the window. "But my perspective's changed having you here."

I shrugged, then started filling a soup pan with water. "It's not that bad."

"You're not the one trying to protect a teenage kid." He gave up with a sigh.

Instead of arguing the many points I could have raised

over that last comment, I focused my energy on ripping open the pasta box.

"You're going to be able to get your learner's permit soon. Maybe I can show you a few pointers."

"Driving?" I asked, remembering it had seemed so all-important last year. Right up until Mom sat me down and said she had pancreatic cancer.

"Yes, driving. Most kids your age can't wait to have a little taste of freedom that four wheels provide." Nick scraped the charred remains into the garbage can. "Anytime you want to go for a spin, I'll volunteer as victim."

I stood in front of the stove, waiting for the water to boil. How was it that saying went?

"Okay, thanks. I'll let you know."

"You got it."

Nick was right. I should start learning to drive. If I followed through with the emancipation, I'd need some way to get myself from point A to point B. Not to mention find a job, and a few dozen other things to prove I was capable of living on my own.

"So what's this with you hanging out with Kel Remington?" The rice pan clattered into the sink with the other one.

My quills rose. "We're not 'hanging out.' I'm tutoring him."

"Yeah, but why do *you* have to tutor *him?*"

I inhaled slowly so I wouldn't say something I shouldn't. "Because I need forty hours of community service for my leadership class. I elected to fill those hours with tutoring, and his name was first on the list."

Nick leaned into the counter and crossed his arms. I kept

staring at the pot. Which was still not boiling. "I'm going to talk to your teacher. Ask about getting you set up with a different student."

"No." It came from nowhere. "I mean, please don't. I don't want my teacher to think I'm too afraid or incapable of handling Kel."

Nick threw his hands into the air. "You *should* be scared of Kel Remington. You shouldn't be 'handling' a guy like him."

"What's that supposed to mean?" I spun around, crossing my arms.

"It means he's the kind of guy no father wants his daughter spending any time around, community service included."

The surge of anger overcame the twist of guilt I could feel rising with my words. "You'd also think no father would ever choose to abandon his daughter, but it happens. You don't get to tell me who gets to be in my life. You haven't earned that privilege."

The instant the words were in the open, I regretted them.

Nick didn't say anything, but the expression on his face alone was enough to tell me how deeply my words had cut. He didn't argue my accusation. He didn't attempt to defend himself. Instead, he nodded his head and left the kitchen.

I didn't move until a while later when the water behind me began to boil.

FAKE IT UNTIL YOU MAKE IT.

Mom's journal was clutched in my hands as I headed toward the cafeteria Monday. At first, I'd thought she was being funny when she'd scratched those words in big letters at the top of a page. Fake it until you make it. Seemed like something a meathead personal trainer in a gym would say to his clients . . . right before they dropped a dumbbell on their head from trying to lift something they couldn't.

One more check of the page I'd bookmarked confirmed it. My mother was a believer in what was perhaps the lamest of cliché sayings ever.

Pausing outside the cafeteria, I leaned into the wall and read what she'd written below in her normal handwriting. No big, blocky letters underlined three times like Fake It Until You Make It was.

Yeah, baby, I know it's a cliché. But it's overused for a reason: because it works.

I snorted, smiling. At least she knew.

After I'm gone, I know how hard it's going to be for you. Losing your mom will only be the beginning of it. A new city. A new school. A new life. It's going to be difficult.

At this point, I realized what a stupid idea it was to stand here and read Mom's dying words to me smack in the middle of my new high school. Sniffing, I rubbed at my eyes with my sleeve, hoping I didn't appear like I was about to cry.

You're not going to feel like making friends. You're not going to feel like going to school. You're not going to feel like crawling out of bed some days. And that's okay. It's okay to not be okay. I promise. But it will get easier, every day a little bit more so. In the meantime, just take it a minute at a time, and act the part until you're back to feeling the part. Don't feel like smiling? Fake it. Don't feel like going outside? Fake it. Don't feel like making new friends? Fake it.

I know I, above all, have placed a high priority on being authentic. There's a place for that. But not when you're in crisis mode. Crisis mode gives you the right to break the rules and do what needs to be done to survive, so that one day, you can get back to thriving.

So, my darling girl, as I pen these last words, part of me is cringing as I'm sure part of you is as well: FAKE IT UNTIL YOU MAKE IT.

My shirtsleeve made another pass over my eyes, my throat burning from the effort of keeping from bawling. I wasn't sure if she was right or wrong; I had no clue if that kind of philosophy would work while I tried to put the pieces of my life back together. But I was going to try.

After zipping the journal back into my bag, I took a few breaths and peeked inside the cafeteria. I didn't have to feel like the nicest, friendliest, most confident girl in this school . . . but I could pretend.

Kel's words rang in my head: *It's all an act. Pick the part you want to play.*

Dang. It was like my mom and he had mind-melded or something. Different ways of saying it, sure, but the overall message was the same.

My gaze roamed from table to table until I found one that was promising. I recognized a couple of the girls from my leadership class, and the others around the table I'd probably seen in passing but weren't in any of my classes. Everyone was smiling, chatting, the occasional laugh . . . promising.

Making a mental image of what the most confident person in existence would look like, I straightened my posture, lifted my head, settled a relaxed smile into place, and started moving, taking easy, fearless steps.

Inside, my heart felt like it was about to explode, but I kept moving forward anyway.

When I stopped behind the one empty chair at the table,

I waited a moment for someone to notice me. They were all too busy dishing about what they'd done over the weekend, though.

"Hi," I blurted, lifting my hand and waving sorta manically. Thankfully, my hyper wave was mostly done by the time their attention shifted my way. How did a person introduce herself to another? What was I going to follow *Hi* up with?

"The past, present, and future walked into a bar." The words burst from me without my brain signing off on its approval. "It was tense," I finished, internally cringing at the guaranteed embarrassment that was coming. Social isolation would seem like a tropical vacation compared to the label I'd just secured for myself: public pariah.

Just as I was expecting five fingers to joust my way and a cackle of laughter to chase me away, Madeline, one of the girls in my leadership class, smiled. "I haven't heard a joke that bad in forever."

I shrugged, smiling like I had intended for the joke to be a flop and also because I wasn't sure what else to do or say. Thankfully, one of the girls jumped in.

"You're in third-period leadership, right? Just moved here?" Allison, the other girl in leadership said, recognition dawning on her face.

"That's me," I said, reminding myself I had a part to play. *Channel confident. Channel Beyoncé*, I chanted to myself.

"You want to have a seat? There's an open spot." Madeline pulled the empty chair out.

"Oh, yeah. Thanks." I dropped into that chair so fast, it was like the offer would expire in five seconds.

"Intros," Allison proclaimed once I was settled. "You already know Madeline and me, and this is Jenna, Caroline, and the male lurker here is Ben." She elbowed the jock-looking guy beside her. "What's your name again? I'm having a brain fart."

"Quinn," I replied. "Quinn Winters."

"That's right! Quinn." Madeline shook her carrot stick at me, eyeing the empty table in front of me. "Do you pack your lunch too?"

Lunch. I'd forgotten to go through the line to get my lunch before sitting down.

"Actually, no." I held my smile, thinking on the fly. "But today's hot lunch looked like stewed internal organs."

Ben grunted. "It smells like stewed internal organs."

"Then here. Share with me." Allison scooted her chair closer, pushing her lunch between us. "Do you like peanut butter and jelly?"

Nothing about my smile was fake anymore. Mom used to make me PB&J's almost daily.

"It's my favorite," I said, taking the other half of Allison's PB&J when she held it toward me. "Thanks."

"Cafeteria scoop." Jenna tipped her head to the side. "Guess who's in trouble again."

Four heads instantly spun in the direction she was focused on. Mine lagged behind.

My face froze when I saw who was being escorted out by not one but two of the high school's security staff. Even being flanked by two grown men, Kel towered over them.

"What's he in trouble for?" I asked, not meaning to say anything at all.

"*This* time?" Jenna clucked her tongue. "Who knows. Could be drugs. Could be a fight. Could be one of a hundred things when it comes to Kel Remington."

My throat did that dry, pained thing again. "So he gets in trouble a lot?"

"Every few weeks," Ben added.

"He came to Riverview a year and a half ago, and he's probably been to the office twenty times. I heard they have a reserved seat for him in there."

"Jenna, don't spread rumors. We don't know *why* Kel gets called to the principal's. Just that he does," chided Allison.

"A lot," Ben muttered.

"Yeah, and how many do-gooders do you see getting hauled into those offices?"

All eyes landed on me, like I was Do-Gooder of the Year or something.

"Do you guys know him at all?" I asked, hoping I didn't sound like I was too interested in all information marked Kel Remington.

"Nobody knows him. Not really. No shortage of girls wanting to get to know him, but yeah . . ." Allison pointed her water bottle in Ben's direction. "He's on the baseball team with Ben. Or *was* last year."

"So you must know him," I said to Ben, who was still watching Kel leave the cafeteria.

"I know he's one hell of a baseball player. He's a big part of the reason we went to state last year. He's also why we probably won't go back this year." Ben adjusted the bill of his baseball cap. "Last I heard, his grades suck so bad there's no way he'll be eligible to play."

"Not to mention his attendance record is close to getting him expelled altogether," Allison chimed in.

"So you guys play on the same team and you don't know him at all?"

Madeline gave me a curious look.

Ben leaned his chair back. "He showed up, he played hard, we won games. That was enough for us. And he was the one who made it clear he wasn't into the whole team-bonding, going-out-and-celebrating-a-win thing."

"He made enemies?" I asked.

Ben's head shook. "Not enemies . . ." His forehead creased as he appeared to be searching for the right word. "Some people are all bark and no bite. They might say they're going to kick your ass, but never will." Ben waved in the direction Kel had disappeared. "Remington's the other type. No bark and *all* bite."

The table was gathering up the remnants of their lunch, but I couldn't let this go yet. "How do you know, though? Has he ever come after you?"

"Hell, no. I haven't given him any reason to," Ben answered.

"All you have to do is take a good look at him every once in a while, Quinn." Madeline waited beside me after she stood up. "It's a rare day when Kel doesn't come to school looking like he's got an after-school job kicking ass for the MMA or something."

"Yeah, and if that's the way a guy like Kel looks after a fight, I'd hate to see the other guy." Allison faked a shudder.

"Only way would be at the city morgue," Ben muttered under his breath.

Finally standing, I shouldered my bag and wandered away from the table with them. It was awesome getting to leave with other humans beside me instead of a wide sweep of open air, but I couldn't shut off the curiosity switch. "Yeah, but none of you know for sure who he really is. It's all just speculation." I aimed an apologetic face at Madeline, but she didn't seem fazed by what I'd said.

"Better to err on the side of caution." Madeline nudged me, pointing at a familiar shadow stepping into the office. "Especially with the likes of Kel Remington."

Never show up to a party empty-handed!
(I know, I know, not life-changing, but
totally practical.)

Why I was lingering in the hallway instead of hauling my butt into sixth was beyond me. I'd never purposely skipped a class. I'd missed days for being sick or after Mom died, and I'd missed classes for doctor's appointments and stuff, but I'd never played hooky.

Yet here I was, about to cross that line for the first time because of a guy . . . which wasn't nearly as interesting as it sounded. We weren't meeting to make out in some supply closet or to go on a joyride—the guy in question didn't even know I was coming. But he was about to.

Kel had skipped sixth period yesterday, and it didn't take a genius to calculate he'd most likely cut today, too. Mr. Johnson didn't need to say it yesterday when his gaze landed on the empty stool Kel normally occupied—Kel was about to flunk chemistry if he didn't start showing up.

The last few stragglers were rushing to their classes as my foot anxiously tapped the ground. Why did I care if Kel skipped class again? I didn't know if he was about to fail or be suspended, but I couldn't get over the urge to step in and interfere with his apparent plans to send his high school career into the trash.

Maybe I was standing here, waiting, because I could recognize a silent cry for help better than most.

When the final bell rang through the halls, I jumped, half expecting to find a team of administrators combing the halls, detention slips in hand. Instead, there was only one person, moving toward the exit.

Right on cue.

Kel didn't notice me following him. He had a hoodie tucked over his head and his hands stuffed into his front pockets. Instead of heading off school grounds, he wandered up the grassy hill in the direction of the sports fields. I had to jog to catch up to him.

"Hey," I panted, coming up beside him.

He didn't flinch like I'd surprised him, though his eyes gave him away. "The bell just rang."

"Oh, so you did hear it. Wasn't sure, since class is that way"—my thumb shot over my shoulder toward the school—"and you're heading in the opposite direction."

"I'm the kid who skips. You're the kid who has a perfect attendance record." Kel's pace slowed when he heard me breathing heavily. "If you hurry, you can keep that flawless record. Mr. Johnson gives first-time offenders a pass."

"Are *you* going back to class?" I asked.

A snort came from Kel. "Does it look like it?"

"Fine, then neither am I." I set my jaw and squared my shoulders.

"Yes, you are." Kel stopped.

My head shook as I kept walking. "You skip, I skip," I sang. "It's my new policy."

Kel's hand found my arm, and his gaze locked on mine. "Hey, smart-ass. I'm not so dumb I can't pick up sarcasm."

My eyebrow rose, a dare as I scooted around him and continued toward where I guessed he'd been heading before I showed up. The grass lining the baseball field was wet from today's rain.

Kel inclined his head in the direction of the dugouts. "If you're going to be out here, you might as well stay dry. So why are you really skipping?" he asked, following me inside the dugout.

"People will find out I'm your tutor, and if you fail classes and get benched, that's going to reflect poorly on me. And that's not fair, because you never even gave me a chance to tutor you, but it will look like *I'm* the failure," I said matter-of-factly, dusting off the bench before taking a seat.

"You've never had to lie much, have you?" When my face lined with confusion, he added, "Because you're not very good at all. And besides, you're not the failure here, I did." He bent forward, resting his arms on his legs, staring at the field.

I inched closer. "Neither are you. Now, are you going to tell me why *you* were skipping class?"

Kel shifted uncomfortably beside me, but I plowed

through. "No? In that case, since we've determined I'm not leaving your side—even if that does tarnish my previously impeccable attendance record—what do you say we get to work? If you won't go to class, I'll bring the classroom to you."

"Can't say I've ever closed down a library before," Kel said as we left the public library a few days later. Riverview High's closed at six, but with baseball practice having started, the only time for tutoring was later in the evening.

"What a rebel you are. Having to be kicked out of a study room by a librarian at nine-oh-one on a school night." I gave a whistle as we wandered down the sidewalk.

"Told you I was trouble."

A laugh snuck past my lips. "With a capital T."

"Hey, thanks for the help." Kel nudged me. "I think I might be able to remember at least enough facts about the Battle of the Somme to not totally bomb my history test tomorrow."

"Dates the battle was fought." I glimpsed over to find his forehead drawn together in concentration.

"July first, 1916, to . . ." Those forehead lines carved deeper. "November . . . mid-November . . . ish," he finished.

I smiled at the sidewalk. "Quoting our history book, November eighteenth, 1916."

He snapped his fingers. "The eighteenth. That's right."

"The Somme River is in which country?" I asked next.

"Easy." He gave me a smug expression. "France."

"How many total casualties?"

He didn't miss a beat. "One point one million."

"And how many square miles of land did the Allies take from the Germans?"

Kel gave a grumble after concentrating for a few seconds. "A lot?"

"One hundred and twenty square miles," I rattled off.

He lifted his arm. "Translation. A lot."

I checked my phone to see if I'd missed any calls or texts. Nada. "History teachers tend to be sticklers for details. You know, in case you sit down at your test tomorrow and consider answering a question with 'a lot' or 'November-ish.' "

"But what's the point, really? We memorize all these meaningless facts that have no real-world application because anyone can do a Google search and find the answer in under thirty seconds. Doesn't make sense to me." Kel's eyes narrowed on something up ahead. I couldn't tell what it was, but he seemed to have a sixth sense that I didn't.

"That, right there, is the question students have been asking since the invention of the encyclopedia. I don't know *why* they make us memorize all this stuff, just that they do."

"Let's go down this street." Kel cut in front of me when we came to the next intersection.

I stopped and shot him a confused look. "But my apartment's down this way."

"We can still get to it from here."

"Yeah, but it'll take forever," I said. When I kept moving down the same street, Kel fell in beside me. Reluctantly.

As we rounded the next block, I began to hear music and voices. It sounded like some kind of party, but there weren't any houses along this stretch of road; just a bunch of closed-up shops and run-down buildings.

Kel's stride picked up as we approached, and at the edge of my vision a few shadows staggered outside what appeared to be an old car wash.

"Remington?! That you?!" a voice crowed from the dark.

Kel quickened his pace even more.

"Hey, I know that's you, man. I recognize the stench of badass when I smell it."

"Do you know them?" I asked, coming to a stop, still trying to see into the darkness.

"No." He paused when he realized I was no longer beside him.

"Then how do they know your name?"

"Because we share the same spot of space on this planet."

"Neighbors?" I guessed. It was already late, but the lure of getting to know more about Kel was too strong to resist. "I want to meet them," I said, already heading toward the run-down car wash.

Kel's hand whipped out to find mine. "Some other time."

"This time is as good as any." Pulling my hand from his grip, I kept going.

I didn't miss the frustrated grumble Kel gave before jogging to catch up with me.

"What do you know? Remington's taking a break from his busy schedule to spend some time slummin' with us." There were a few guys circled around a rusted-out metal drum, where a small fire was burning. They looked about our age, maybe a little older, but they all had that same dulled gleam in their eyes like Kel; as though they'd seen enough to be twice their actual age.

"And who's this?" a boy with a black ball cap asked, making room for Kel and me to circle up around the burn barrel.

"Nobody I'm introducing to a joke like you—"

"I'm Quinn," I said, shooting Kel a look. "Kel and I go to school together."

The one with the oversized sweatshirt bounced his brows at me. "Anything else you and Kel do together?"

"Yeah," I said, refusing to let him get a rise from me. "We study."

"I need to get me a study partner." The boy elbowed the one next to him. "What does a fool like you need to study for, anyways, Remington?"

Kel shoved the kid playfully, but making a point, too: I was not to be messed with. "Okay, I'm doing introductions only because Quinn here asked, not because I actually think any of you deserve to meet her."

"Of course she asked. She knows the goods when she sees them." The boy brushed his shoulders all showy like, popping off a wink at the same time.

Kel rolled his neck. "Jackson, Matt, and Deon." He pointed at each one as he rattled off their names. When he was finished, he glanced at me like he was hoping we could leave now.

"You seem like a nice girl, Quinn. So what are you doing hanging around a guy like Remington?" Matt asked.

I wiped my face of all expression. "I'm a glutton for punishment."

A chorus of jeers came at Kel, but he just shook his head, mildly amused at my burn.

"Everyone else is inside." Deon indicated a half-open garage door leading into the car wash behind them. "Why don't you and Quinn go say hey?"

"Nah, we've got to get go—" Kel started, but I interrupted.

"Great—I'd love to meet them."

I made for the car wash before Kel could find some excuse to leave, the music volume increasing with every step. The bass beat felt like a gong banging inside my chest. With only a moment's hesitation to consider the dilapidated mess around us, I ducked into the building.

Once inside, I just stood there for a minute, taking everything in. There were a couple dozen people stationed around a clearly gutted car wash. There were a few hoses and brushes left, but everything else had been removed. It felt more like a big concrete garage.

Kel appeared at my side. "This isn't a good idea, Quinn," he said, shifting every few seconds.

No one seemed to pay us much attention, but a few heads turned, cups tipping in Kel's direction. A few kids were smoking toward the back, and couples were gyrating, but nothing too crazy. Teens having fun, letting off a little steam. Might have been a bit above my rebel grade, but no records were being set at the Suds N Soak Car Wash tonight.

"It's fine, Kel. These are your people?" I asked him, then remembered Mrs. Guthrie's term. "Your tribe?"

Kel choked on a laugh. "No. God, no." He followed as I began weaving my way through the room. "Like I said, we're victims of circumstance." He read the quizzical look on my face. "We live in the same subsidized housing sprawl."

"Oh."

"Sorry to break it to you that I'm not a trust fund kid. Shocker, I know."

I snorted. "Yeah, me either."

I watched a couple in the center of the room, their limbs so tangled I wasn't sure how they'd come undone. My cheeks flamed as they moved in rhythm. "You wanna dance?" I motioned over to the dance floor.

Kel's eyes widened at me. "Do *you* want to dance?"

I nodded my head microscopically, but it was enough.

Kel's fingers brushed against mine and our fingers braided together as he pulled me into the throng.

His other hand found its way to me, his body positioning against mine with the kind of confidence that came from experience. My body was the opposite—completely unsure what to do or where to put my hands.

Fighting a smile, Kel took my hands and settled them over his shoulders. Then his fingers dropped to my hips, drawing me close enough that his chest brushed mine every time he inhaled. When he started to move, I did my best to keep up with his movements, mirroring his tempo.

Tingles scattered across my scalp, leaving a trail all the way down to my toes as we moved across the floor. I'd danced with other guys before, but dancing with Kel . . . it was completely different. My heart was beating hard, and he was so close, I was worried he could hear it, even above the pulse of the music. His head dropped beside mine, the ends of his hair brushing my temple. I felt him lean in, pulling me closer still as if to say something. Then he tensed.

"Hey, Remington. You forgot something last time I saw you." A voice startled me from my reverie. Someone had appeared beside Kel.

Kel's jaw tightened as he turned toward the newcomer. "What's that, McAllister?"

Without warning the guy swung his arm. "This." His fist connected with Kel's jaw, sending him backward into the wall.

I cried out in surprise, but before I could see if Kel was okay, he sprang off the wall toward McAllister, crashing into him with shocking force. For a moment, I'd forgotten how big Kel was, and the anger in his eyes terrified me. The fight was drawing a crowd, and people crammed in, forming a ring in front of me. I began shoving between bodies toward the frenzy. The music was still thumping in the background, but the sounds of fists connecting and grunts overpowered it.

"Stop!" I shouted, barreling toward Kel. I'd never seen a fight like this before. It seemed like they were killing each other. "Enough!" I forced my way between Kel and McAllister.

But McAllister's fist came first, landing smack into my cheek.

I yelped as I crashed to the ground, my hand going to my cheek.

I don't know who was more stunned: me or McAllister. But there was no contest for who was the most pissed.

"I'm going to kill you!" Kel charged at McAllister but was intercepted by a few other guys, who tackled him against the wall behind him.

"McAllister, get your sorry ass out of here." Jackson got into McAllister's face, corralling him toward the exit. McAllister stopped fighting them.

Behind me, I could still hear Kel struggling against the guys holding him back, but the fight in him was draining.

"Let me go."

"Once you cool down, man," one of the guys replied. "Don't need you chasing down McAllister for round two."

"To hell with McAllister," Kel rumbled. "Quinn? Dammit. Are you okay? How bad is it?"

"I'll survive," I assured him, watching as his face transformed from anger to concern. My head shook in an effort to release some of the shock I felt from having just been punched in the face by a guy twice my size. "And I look a heck of a lot better than you." Just glancing at his face made me grimace in commiseration.

"Would you let me go already? I'm cool." Kel raised his hands at last, breaking the guys' hold.

He crouched down beside me, his face burdened with worry, a trickle of blood streaming from one nostril. "Ah, shit, Quinn. This is my fault."

"It wasn't your fist that my face got in the way of."

"Might as well have been." His fingers lightly brushed my swollen cheek. "Does it hurt?"

"Only a little," I said, even though it hurt more than a little. I didn't want to make him feel any worse than he already did.

"You need ice." He was already rising, heading toward the exit.

"I'm fine. Really."

"No, you're not. Wait here." He didn't say anything else before ducking through the door. The tears began forming as I watched him go.

"That's going to be one hell of a shiner." Deon gave a whistle.

Jackson made a face when he took a good look at me. "Yeah, you are one tough mother."

"Um. Thanks?" I managed to choke out.

Just then, a racket sounded outside, and someone stuck their head into the car wash. "Po-po!" he shouted.

My mind hiccuped over what that meant, but everyone else sprang into action. Bodies rushed toward the door, sprinting from the garage.

I stood, and a jolt of pain shot through my head, making my vision blur. Blinking wildly, I fumbled my way toward the exit. Everyone else had vanished, but I could still hear the shouts and scuffle coming from outside.

I ran toward the sound and was almost to the opening when a beam of light landed on my face. "Hold it right there."

Nick did not look happy. In fact, he was full-on irate.

"I can't believe you, Quinn" were the first words from his mouth once we were inside the truck. "I don't even know what to say right now." His hand slammed the dashboard so hard, I worried it might break. "What do you have to say for yourself?"

My head ached from more than just the punch. Getting put into the back seat of a cruiser and waiting for my "guardian" to come claim me was enough to induce a blinding migraine.

"I'm sorry," I started, rubbing at my temples. "I didn't mean to—"

"Get caught?" Nick interrupted.

My head settled against the side window. "Inconvenience you."

Whatever he was about to say caught in his throat. For a minute.

"You're lucky that was a security guard instead of the police."

I nodded, dying to crawl into my bed and put this whole night behind me.

"You're lucky no one's pressing charges."

"I know," I said under my breath.

"You're lucky something worse than that shiner on your cheek didn't happen to you, hanging around with that bunch of nobodies—"

"Yeah." I bit at the inside of my cheek. "I know how *lucky* I am."

Nick's leg was bouncing as we rode down the quiet streets. "I can't believe you did this, Quinn. You've never acted this way."

My head began pounding anew. "How would you know? You missed the past ten years!" The words erupted without consent, making me sit up in my seat.

"Now is *not* the time to be throwing that in my face, Quinn." Nick's grip tightened around the steering wheel. "I am in *no* mood."

We pulled up to the apartment a minute later. As Nick maneuvered the truck into a parking spot, I noticed a dark shadow lingering beneath a streetlight.

Kel had his hood drawn over his head, his eyes never leaving the ground.

"Oh, hell no." Nick punched the truck into park, glaring through the windshield at Kel.

I threw open my door and jumped outside before Nick could get to him, unsure what he'd do to Kel if he got him in arm's reach.

"You. Leave. Now." Nick spoke coldly to Kel as he climbed from the truck.

Kel shoved off the lamppost, angling toward us. "I just wanted to check on Quinn."

Nick huffed. "You've done more than enough for one night. Now leave, before I call the police."

"Nick," I hissed.

Kel moved a little closer. "Quinn, I'm so sorry. When I found out what happened . . . Are you okay?"

Nick put himself in front of me. "Of course she's not okay. I just got called at work to come pick up my daughter for trespassing on private property, and I get there to find one side of her face swelling up to the size of a grapefruit. How is that anything close to okay?"

Kel's eyes closed, his sneaker toeing at the sidewalk.

"I'm all right. Really," I added.

"I shouldn't have put you in that situation."

"Damn right you shouldn't have—"

"*I* put myself in that situation," I said. "You were the one who tried talking me out of it."

"It's late. You need to get to bed, and *you* need to get home." Nick waved Kel off as he steered me toward the apartment entrance. "Do us all a favor and stop dragging Quinn into your trouble."

Be grateful. You cannot be unhappy and grateful at the same time. Universal law.

I'd just gotten settled on the couch, with my spread of poster board and markers so I could make a Tigers baseball schedule to put up in the cafeteria, when the sound of a key turning over in the lock came earlier than I was expecting it.

"Homework?" Nick gave a quick glance at my spread on the couch. Things were still tense after the car wash incident, but Nick had calmed down after I swore to him this was my first time getting into real trouble. He grounded me for a week but made it clear that if it happened again, my next sentence would be a year.

"Yeah, a leadership project," I said, yanking off the red marker's cap. "I didn't think you'd be back until your usual time."

He carried the paper sack in his arms into the kitchen. "I didn't work tonight. I took it off."

"Oh. Do you do that often? Take a night off?" It was the first one he hadn't worked since I'd moved in.

"Not very, but every once in a while, I take a vacation day."

"What do you do on your vacation days?" I asked automatically as I carried my backpack into my room. Once it was tucked beside my bed, hidden from view, I could breathe again.

"Nothing too exciting. Get together with a few buddies. Sometimes we bowl, or grab a bite to eat, or whatever."

I nodded.

When his gaze shifted in my direction, I slid some hair over my face where the bruise was fading but still apparent. Every time Nick stared at it, he got this guilty look on his face, like it was his fault I'd tried stopping a fight with my face.

"Hey, I've been thinking." Nick leaned into the kitchen doorway. "You've got to miss your friends back in Leavenworth. You probably miss lots of things back there." His arms folded when he shifted, visibly uncomfortable. "Why don't we plan a day I could drive you over there? Pick a date and we'll make it happen. We could get there early so you could have all day to catch up with friends. . . ."

I considered telling Nick about Raven's party.

Then his throat cleared. "And, ya know, visit your mom's grave."

My lungs collapsed, hearing him mention it. Mention *her*. "I don't think that's a good idea."

The skin between Nick's brows creased. "Really?" he said, confused. "I thought you'd give anything to go back."

My eyes burned as I clutched my knees to my chest. He was trying to connect. "I *do* want to go home." My voice shook, but it didn't break. "But I'm not ready to see it again. The cemetery."

It took a few moments for my words to sink in. "It was just an idea. You wouldn't need to go to the cemetery. You could do other stuff."

My mind was running away, emotions flicking the whip to keep it charging ahead. Mom. Grave. Cold. Empty. Alone. I broke out in a cold sweat. Dropping the blanket, I went for the door to get some fresh air.

Nick's hand raised as he shoved off the doorway. "Quinn, honey, are you okay?"

My lip quivered as my hand curled around the doorknob. "I need to be alone right now."

"It's almost nine o'clock at night."

"I can't . . ." Words lodged in my throat. I felt the apartment closing in around me. Before Nick could respond, I charged through the door in my pajamas and slippers.

"Quinn!" Nick's voice echoed behind me, but I raced onto the dark sidewalk. I ran down the road. The sidewalks were damp from another day of ceaseless rain, but thankfully, my slippers had sturdy rubber bottoms.

By the time my legs and lungs gave out a few blocks later, my mind had almost cleared. I knew Nick would be furious. I probably really would be grounded for a year now, but I couldn't stay in that apartment.

I was passing the parking lot when I realized my aimless journey had taken me to the high school. The parking lot was empty, the school dark. Not yet ready to go back,

I checked for a place to decompress. My feet led me toward the dugout.

The soles of my slippers squished along the walkway when I heard my cell phone ping. A message from Nick came through. **Where are you?**

Out. I typed back.

He responded immediately. **Quinn, I need to make sure you're safe. Come home.** "You have *got* to possess the survival instincts of a dodo," a voice announced from the dark up ahead.

Instead of turning and running, I froze. Further confirming those survival instincts.

"I heard you coming from home plate and was checking to see what badass was creeping nearby, and I find you." I was able to hear the smirk in his voice, though I couldn't see it in the dark. "Alone. At night." Then Kel came into view.

I smiled in recognition, sending one more text to Nick. **I'm safe. Promise. I'm with a friend and will be home soon. But Renton is not my home.** I switched my phone to silent and put it away. When I looked up, I was surprised to find Kel's smirk had given way to concern.

"What are you doing out here, Quinn?"

I worked to unfreeze my body. "Walking," I said, all matter-of-fact.

Kel's arms crossed. "Let me rephrase that—don't think I got my intended message across." His throat cleared as he came closer. "What *in the hell* are you doing out here, Quinn?"

"Walking," I repeated.

Kel sighed as he adjusted a duffel he had slung across his

back. I could see the end of a baseball bat jutting from it. "You're being stupid." He motioned at me, like I was proving his point. "You have no sense of self-preservation. I thought you would have learned your lesson after the car wash." He grimaced when he eyed my bruised cheek. Like Nick, Kel couldn't stare at it without seeming like he was swallowing glass shards. He'd kept his distance after that night. He'd barely looked at me in class—when he'd bothered to show up at all. And he'd stopped coming to tutoring altogether. This was the first time I'd been within arm's length of him since then. "Come on, what are you doing?"

My jaws ground together from being lectured like I was some little kid. "I could ask you the same question." I blinked at him as he stepped into the glow from the streetlamps.

He gazed behind his shoulder at his bag. "Batting practice."

"By yourself? Isn't it kinda late for that? Seems like you need to actually see the ball if you're going to hit it." My arms folded over my chest when I remembered I wasn't wearing a bra. And it was chilly. And, well . . . yeah.

To Kel's credit, his gaze hadn't drifted south of my face.

"Not if you're able to see in the dark."

"That's right." My eyes rolled. "You *are* the dark."

"Nice of you to remember." His hand settled on my shoulder, gently turning me around and giving a nudge. "Now, shining star, get home where you belong."

"I'm not going back there." My eyes dropped instantly. I hadn't intended to say anything.

"Quinn?" He stepped up beside me, lowering his head to mine. "What happened?"

"Nick and I . . . ," I began.

"Did you get into a fight?" he interrupted.

"No," I answered. "Not really."

"Is there tension between you two because of me?" he asked. "Because if I'm the reason, I get why he's concerned. He's just looking out for his daughter. There's nothing wrong with a dad wanting what's best for his kid."

My feet stopped moving. Maybe in some supersmall way, Kel had a point. Could it be that Nick wanted what was best for me, and by default, *cared* about me?

I pushed away the thought.

"Listen, it's not a big deal," I said, shuffling down the sidewalk again. "I'll be fine."

"You're not fine right now." His hand motioned in my direction. "And you'll be even less fine if you wander down the wrong street this time of night."

"You keep acting like I'm surrounded by danger."

Kel fell in beside me. "You are. Have you learned nothing from the other night?"

"You're not dangerous."

Kel said nothing.

"Fine, you're the big, bad wolf? Is that it?"

In answer, he held out his arms and did a slow spin.

"And what am I?"

His fingers brushed the sleeve of my crimson T-shirt. "Little Red Riding Hood."

"You do realize the wolf winds up destroying Red, right?"

The easy smile slowly receded, the light in Kel's eyes wavering. "I know how it ends."

A few moments passed, nothing but the sounds of the city filling in the quiet.

"Do you still talk to your friends back home?" he asked.

Thinking about them made that tiny knife permanently embedded in my heart twist. "All the time."

"Why don't you go visit them sometime? Isn't Leavenworth only a few hours' drive from here?"

"I'm going to. Soon, hopefully. One of my good friends has a birthday party coming up and I'm trying to swing getting over there. But my transportation options are pretty much nonexistent," I said, scuffing the sidewalk with the toe of my slipper.

"What about your dad?"

I huffed. "Not an option."

"There's buses that go through there all the time." Kel adjusted the bag on his shoulder, scanning the streets.

"That cost forty bucks a pop each way."

Kel was quiet for a minute, the corners of his eyes creasing like he was working something out. "What if you had a friend who had access to a vehicle?"

My mouth pulled at the corners. "I'd ask if this friend had a license."

"He does."

"A *valid* one."

Kel rolled his neck, fighting a smile. "Does it matter?"

I gave that a moment's thought. It didn't require much. "Really?" I half-exclaimed. "You'd do that?"

"Of course I would," he replied, making a face like it was no big deal. Even though it was a very huge deal.

"Thank you so much." I was almost bouncing down the sidewalk now, but when the next gust of wind hit me, I shivered.

"My place isn't too much farther. We can crash there for a little while until you're ready to head back to yours." Kel's hands pulled up into fists, relaxed, then repeated. "I'll walk you back when you are."

"I want to keep walking." I got back to rubbing at my arms, checking to make sure they were still covering cold-sensitive parts of my chest.

"You can keep walking, but I'm coming with you. Seriously, you don't know this neighborhood. You shouldn't be here. Plus your lips turned purple two blocks ago. You have to get inside soon before they fall off or something. If you don't want to go to my place, we can go to a pizza place or coffee shop or something." He pointed across the street to the pizza place, already steering me that direction.

"No." I kept my feet anchored in place, noting all the occupied tables through the pizza shop's glass windows. "Your place works."

Kel glanced at me, like he was giving me a chance to change my mind . . . or maybe like he was *hoping* I would. I didn't, though. Being around a couple of people was better than an entire restaurant full.

"It's not far." He moved down the sidewalk, his movements stiff. Like he was bracing himself.

"Are you sure it's okay? It's late and I don't want your mom to be upset when she finds a girl in her living room on a school night. In her pajamas," I added.

"It'll be fine. She'll be passed out by now anyway."

I had to hustle to keep up with him. Now that he was moving, he was hauling. I followed his gaze to an apartment building up ahead. It seemed as though he was angling himself in front of me as we neared the building, like he was shielding me from it.

As we got closer, I could understand why. It wasn't exactly

the kind of place a person thought of when they pictured a warm, inviting home. There were a few clusters of guys chilling in front of the first-floor apartments, a few I recognized from the get-together at the car wash. There was some definitely questionable activity happening in the parking lot.

The "lawn" had been trampled down to patches of dirt and a few clumps of crabgrass bursting through. Kids' toys were scattered around, mixed in with garbage and broken lawn chairs. Half the windows on the first floor had some kind of crack webbed through them, jagged lines of duct tape tracing the fractures. That was only a part of it, though— there were also the smells . . . sounds . . .

This apartment complex made the one Nick and I lived in feel like Buckingham Palace.

"Hey, hey, Kel. What's up, brother?" one of the guys in the group we were passing hollered. When he gawked at me, I felt the urge to squirm, but I didn't.

"Looks like you went fishing on the other side of town."

"Isn't it past your bedtime, Nando?" Kel replied coolly, never losing his pace. But I didn't miss how he checked me from the corner of his eye, ever so slightly gliding closer.

"I call dibs when you're done with her, man!"

Kel's jaw worked, but he kept moving. "For someone still recovering from the last ass beating I gave you, you're sure begging for another."

I crept a little closer to Kel. "Nice friends."

"They're not friends." When Kel stopped outside an apartment, I bumped into him thanks to lurking on his heels. "Sorry."

"I got you, Red." He smirked over at me as he unlocked

the door. "Don't worry. None of these wolves will put a hand on you with me around."

"Thanks" was all I could get out. I was too shaken to even formulate a snarky comment about the newest nickname.

Kel's grin fell as he started twisting the doorknob. "We'll have to be quiet. *Really* quiet, 'kay?"

"Okay," I whispered.

Kel stuck his head in, checking the apartment first before slipping inside. He held the door open for me, grabbing my wrist when I began to move from the doorway. "Wait for me."

After closing the door, he locked it, and we stood there inside the entry for a minute, listening. I wasn't sure what we were listening for.

"Kel?" I whispered.

"Just making sure Mom's asleep," he whispered back. "Um, so yeah. Why don't we head into the kitchen? I'll make you something warm to drink so you don't freeze to death." Kel held his arm out, part guiding, part shepherding me into the kitchen right off the hall.

"I'm not that cold," I said, taking in the whole place. I could tell he was uncomfortable with me being at his apartment.

"Your lips are blue. I bet if I touched them, they'd shatter."

My cheeks warmed.

"Why are you so concerned with my lips?"

"Because I just am." His gaze dropped to my mouth, his expression tortured. "Do you like tea? Hot chocolate?" His forehead lined as he dug through a couple of shelves before moving on to the next cupboard. This one was almost as bare as the first. The cupboards might have been empty, but they were the only part of the kitchen that was. Dirty dishes were overflowing from the sink, spilling onto the counter. Empty to-go containers—and maybe some not-so-empty ones, from the smell of things—sat balanced on whatever semiflat surface could be found. The floor was dirty, the walls in the same condition. Not that Nick was a neat freak, but boy, this almost made it seem like he was in comparison.

When Kel reached the last cupboard and found it empty, he cursed under his breath. "How about some hot water?" he said, a little embarrassed.

It was actually kind of refreshing to see this part of him. His home. It explained more about him than he ever had with words.

"Hot water." I made a yum sound. "My favorite."

"Yeah, sorry. I guess Mom didn't make it to the grocery store today." He flipped on the faucet, spinning the handle to the hot side.

"Hey, if I didn't do the grocery shopping at my apartment, Nick and I'd probably both starve." I rested against the fridge, trying to seem at ease. But every time Kel checked over at me, it was as if nothing about me being here was natural. "Maybe you could ask your mom if you could pitch in on grocery shopping duty one day."

"Ah, yeah. Maybe sometime. Sorry it's not hot chocolate."

"My frozen lips thank you." I smiled before taking a drink. I felt its warmth spread through me right away, down into my core, pushing into my chilled extremities.

Kel and I stood like that in the kitchen for a while, his

fingers tapping over the counter ledge while I sipped the rest of the hot water.

"Should we sit?" I scanned for a place to set the empty cup down. There wasn't a patch of bare counter or sink, so I turned it upside down and balanced it on top of an empty vodka bottle.

"Sit down?" Kel rolled his head, checking around the corner. "Yeah, sure." He led the way into the living area. When we passed a couple of doors, he paused to close one of them all the way.

"Sorry it's so messy." Kel scooped some clothes up from the couch and carried them over to an empty laundry basket leaned against a wall. "Mom hasn't been feeling well lately."

"It's okay," I said, taking a seat on the edge of the couch. "I don't mind."

Kel shot a doubtful look my way as he collected some empty bottles and empty food containers from around the room, carrying them toward the sliding glass door. Pulling it open, he carried the trash outside.

With him temporarily gone from the apartment, I scanned the room, finding it in the same condition as the kitchen. It was like a massive party had been thrown and the cleaning crew had forgotten to show up. There was an odor in the air too, a mixture of stale, rot, and an earthy, grassy scent that I'd smelled every July when the hippie convention rolled into Leavenworth.

"Oh, sorry." Kel had made it back inside and was rushing toward me. "I'll move those."

When he motioned at the space beside me, I found a couple of blankets and a pillow stacked neatly.

"Does your mom have a boyfriend on couch detail or something?" I guessed as I handed him the stack of bedding.

Kel huffed, carrying the stack toward a yellowed outdoor table stuffed in the corner. "I sleep on the couch, actually."

I shifted. "You do? Why?"

Kel kept his back toward me as he answered. "There's only one bedroom in the apartment."

"I know the feeling," I muttered.

"Yeah, we move a lot, so sometimes I have a bedroom, sometimes I don't."

"How many times have you moved?" I asked, trying to get comfortable on the couch.

"Six times? Seven?" His shoulders lifted. "I've lost count."

"Why all the upheaval?"

"Why does anyone leave?" he asked, like the answer was obvious.

"For a fresh start?"

A sharp exhale came from him. "Or to escape a rotten past."

I was about to ask what he meant when Kel's fists clenched. "Dammit!" he hissed under his breath, shoving aside the bedding on the table in a frenzied manner.

"What?" I leapt off the couch, striding toward him.

I found an array of papers and a couple of textbooks, right beside a toppled-over jug of some amber-colored alcohol. It was mostly empty now, its contents absorbed by the papers and books.

"It's okay." I righted the bottle and scooted it away as Kel pounded his fist down.

"My algebra homework is soaked in whiskey, Quinn.

Pretty sure that's not part of the assignment." Kel worked at one of the soaked papers, peeling it off the table.

Most of the assignment was already done—the answers were right, too, I saw when I gave them a quick check. "You did your homework for once?"

Kel shook the drenched paper. "And this is what happens when I do. The universe takes a piss on it." He curled it up, wringing it out on the table below.

"I didn't know the universe had eighty-proof piss." My response caught him off guard and diffused some of his anger.

"I just discovered two days' worth of schoolwork marinating in cheap whiskey and you're making jokes now?" One corner of his mouth twitched.

"Seemed like a healthier option than launching the table through the window."

His shoulders relaxed and he took a breath. "Healthier, maybe, but not as satisfying, trust me."

"I'll take your word for it," I said, reaching for the algebra assignment in his hand. "Let's salvage these." I grabbed a few more papers before heading to the heater wall unit.

"What are you doing? The garbage is the other direction."

"Drying them," I answered as I kneeled in front of the heater and spread the papers on the carpet in front of it.

"They're ruined, Quinn."

"Not *totally* ruined. Take the advice of your tutor." I glanced over at him. "You can still turn them in."

"Reeking of alcohol?"

"It's not like your teachers can dock you points because your homework got tanked one night."

Kel snorted, peeling the last few pages from the table. "Still with the jokes. I didn't know you had a sense of humor, Red."

"My humor doesn't extend into the lame nickname category. Last warning." I shot a no-nonsense look at him as he settled beside me and laid out his sheets with the others.

We sat like that quietly for a while before Kel waved at the room. "Bet you're really wishing you'd gone with the pizza or coffee option now, aren't you?"

My eyes wandered the apartment again before ending on him settled beside me. Kel was more than his reputation and the rumors that circulated Riverview High.

Leaning into him, my head fell heavy onto his shoulder. He tensed instantly but didn't slide away. He stayed right beside me. "I made the right choice."

Never buy underwear unless they come sealed in a package.

Think about it.

"I can smell my paper from here," Kel whispered over at me during the last few minutes of sixth period.

I eyed the stack of homework we'd turned in at the beginning of class. Kel's was clearly rippled with a slight brown tint to it.

"Did you see Mr. Johnson's face? He wouldn't have cared if your homework had poison spikes sticking out of it." Mr. Johnson gave us the warning stare but didn't break stride in his lecture.

Kel moved close enough that I could just detect the scent of his soap. "Turning in a boozy piece of homework. My greatest accomplishment yet."

I smiled at the whiteboard Mr. Johnson was scribbling

on, praying Kel didn't notice the way my skin had prickled when he'd come closer.

After hanging at his place awhile longer last night, Kel took me home. His mom never emerged from her room. I knew having me over had made him uncomfortable, but I didn't know how to tell him that it shouldn't. That I understood. That I knew what it was like to feel like you were out of place in your very own life.

When the bell rang, Kel lingered in his seat as I packed up my bag. "Want me to walk you home?"

I threw my bag on. "Don't you have practice?"

Kel stood with me. "Yeah, but you don't live far and I can haul ass back. We have a half hour once school's done before we have to be on the field anyway."

"Thanks for the offer, but I think I can manage less than a mile on my own," I said as we headed for the door.

"Did you and your dad talk at all?" Kel asked once we were in the hall.

My nose wrinkled. Nick had been asleep when I'd gotten home last night, and I'd taken off this morning before he was awake. It was a chicken move, I knew, but I wasn't ready to confront him after running away last night.

"Nope."

"Are you going to?" he pressed.

"Not planning on it," I answered, focusing on the doors up ahead.

"Maybe you should try. He seems like a decent guy."

My "dad" thinks you are a very undecent guy.

"We still on for tutoring tomorrow night?" he asked as a stream of students emerged from behind, breaking around us. "I've got our first game tomorrow, but it should wrap up around seven." He paused, his eyes shining at me. "If that's not past your bedtime."

My nostrils flared. "I don't have a bedtime."

"I know Red doesn't, but what time is Quinn's?"

When I slugged him, he didn't flinch. Like he'd been expecting it or was used to people landing unexpected hits. "Congratulations," I said. "You've hit your annoying quota for the day. I'm leaving now."

When I turned to take off, Kel called, "You wanna come watch tomorrow?"

My feet stopped moving. "Your game?"

"Well, me and, you know, the rest of my team, along with the opposing one."

"Is there a decent chance I'll get to watch you lose? I think some humility would do you good."

His arms lifted at his sides. "If I did, it would be the first game I ever have."

"You're that good?"

"I'm just one guy. It's a group effort."

My head shook as I kept going. "I think I liked you better when you gave me the silent treatment."

Kel's laugh rumbled behind me. "So I'll see you at the game tomorrow?"

What was I doing? "Maybe."

Nick went to work earlier than usual on Thursdays, so I had the apartment to myself and could put off our inevitable "talk" a few hours longer. Once inside, I headed straight for my room. I wanted to change into something comfy before diving into my homework. Some of the leadership kids were heading into Seattle for a concert and had invited me, but I'd taken a pass. It was nice having a few new friends, but I didn't want to press my luck with Nick. Asking for ticket money and permission to head into the city with a bunch of kids I'd just met? He might have been chill about a lot of things, but I was pretty sure this request would not go over well.

Gliding the curtain aside to enter my bedroom, I froze. This wasn't my bedroom.

Checking, I found the same curtains hung around the same space, but everything else had changed. Different bed and blankets, different nightstand, different *everything*.

A couple of pairs of worn work boots were lined up beneath the bed—that's what gave away whose stuff had replaced mine. Wandering past the curtains, I headed toward Nick's room. The door was partly open, a big purple bow taped to the center of it along with a note that read, I know it'll never replace Leavenworth, but I hope someday Renton can be home too.

Shoving the door open, I took a moment to realize what I was seeing. My bed, blankets, storage containers, personal items had all been moved in here. The room smelled like cleaner; there were lines in the carpet from being freshly vacuumed.

Everything of Nick's had been taken from the room to make space for my stuff. Except for one thing.

The photo of Mom and me was still here, propped next to the other photos I'd brought with me from Leavenworth.

My eyes burned when I stepped inside, staring at that picture of Mom holding me as a baby. I wasn't sure why Nick had left it here. Maybe he was trying to let go of the past or perhaps he figured the picture would mean more to me than it did to him. I knew so little about the man who was my father, but as I crossed the floor into my new room and took a seat on my bed, I realized I knew more about him now than I had when I'd first arrived.

And I liked what I was getting to know.

"Baseball? You're not going to tell the umpire to shove his bad calls where the sun doesn't shine again, are you?" Meg asked on the other end of the phone as I got in line at the concession stand next to the high school's fields.

"Ha. Ha. Not funny," I said, checking the menu options. I was starving, and baseball games weren't known for their brevity.

"Riverview High have a decent baseball team?"

"I'm about to find out." Moving up in line, I weeded a couple of dollars from my bag.

"High school ball, though, eh? I thought you were more of an MLB fan. Extra-credit assignment for leadership, right?" Meg was at track practice. I could hear the whistles and shouts of coaches in the background, but she'd still answered my call when it came in.

"Um, well . . ." I stalled, not sure what to tell her. "Actually I'm here watching a friend play."

There was a bloated silence on the other end. "A friend?" Only Meg could make such a tame word sound scandalous.

"And since this is baseball instead of softball, I take it this 'friend' is a boy?"

"Yeah, he's a boy." My eyes squeezed shut when I heard myself. "One I have a class with and am helping tutor."

"What exactly are you tutoring him in?" Judging from her voice, Meg's smile was diabolical.

"You are so immature."

"You are so blushing right now."

My foot stomped when I realized she was right. My cheeks were seriously heated. "So, yeah, I'm going to let you get back to track practice. Wouldn't want to deprive you of running twelve hundred miles or whatever Coach K has planned to torture you with today."

"Not so fast. You're the one who called me." The noise in the background dimmed, so she must have been ducking beneath the bleachers or something. "Who is this boyfriend? I want details. *Fine* details." My head shook as she kept going. "Starting with height, weight, and gait."

"Gait?" I rubbed at my forehead, rethinking my phone call.

"Swagger level," she said, all matter-of-fact like. "Gait."

When it was my turn, I pointed at a licorice rope and some M&M's. The afternoon snack of champions. "Uh, I don't know. He's tall. I don't know how to answer the other two."

"Tall and built? Or tall and wiry?"

I took my candy and change and scooted aside so no one had to be subjected to this idiotic conversation. "Tall and built. I guess."

Megan made a sound on the other end. Part squee, part

whoop. "Gait? Swagger factor?" she added, like I'd already forgotten.

"Meg, god, I don't know. What does that even matter?"

"It might not matter to you, but it matters to me," she stated. "I'll only allow you to date a guy who has a satisfactory amount of swagger."

"You should really get back to track practice. We can check in later tonight."

"Not so fast. One more thing."

I groaned, ripping open my M&M's to ease the pain. "What?"

"Name." When I stayed quiet, she sang, "I've got all afternoon, baby. I wasn't really feeling like running twelve hundred miles today anyway."

"Kel," I blurted.

"Huh?"

I sighed. "Kel," I repeated, slower this time.

"Kel . . ."

"Remington," I said. "Kel Remington."

Megan whistled on the other end. "Name's got swagger, that's for sure."

"Well, thanks for the words of wisdom, but I'm going to go reconsider my life choices right now. Specially bringing up a boy and thinking we could have a mature conversation."

"Ah, sweetie. You're so welcome." Megan made a kissing sound on the other end. "Do me a favor and snap a pic of Super Swagger, would you? Preferably when he's up at bat and you've got a good view of his backside. Please and thank you."

"I'm hanging up now." I popped a handful of M&M's into my mouth.

"Love you too," she sang before ending the call.

Grumbling to myself, I stuffed my phone into my pocket and searched the baseball field. The teams were warming up, Riverview High's black and blue colors a stark contrast to the other team's white and yellow uniforms.

I didn't have a clue what number Kel was, or what position he played, but he was easy to find. He was the one who made the rest of the players on the field look like they were still playing peewee ball.

Why had I agreed to come, again?

Because I was determined to make my life harder than it already was. Oh yeah, that's right. Nice to have the reminder.

Pushing off the concession stand wall, I wandered toward the field. The rain had stopped around lunchtime, but the bleachers were still wet. I was contemplating sitting on my backpack to keep my butt dry when the chain-link fence behind me clinked.

"Here, use this."

As soon as I turned around, Kel tossed a small towel over the fence at me.

I caught it. With my face.

"Thanks," I muttered through the towel before pulling it off my face.

"Nice catch." Kel grinned.

I gave him a tight smile in return and wiped a patch of bleacher dry. I'd never seen him in anything besides his usual oversized T-shirt and dark jeans. A baseball uniform fit him nicely. A little too nicely.

"Thanks," I said again, tossing the towel back over the fence. When it smacked him right back in the face, he shot me an impressed grin.

"Whoa. Are you double-fisting candy?" Kel's gaze dropped to my hands. "You seem so . . . responsible."

"I am responsible, and I like candy." I twirled my licorice rope. "What's the problem?"

Kel's fingers curled through the fence, his grin holding. "Just when I think I have you figured out, you pick licorice and M&M's for an after-school snack."

"What can I say? I'm a real enigma." I moved toward the fence, shaking the packet of M&M's. He squeezed part of his hand between the links.

He pulled his fingers back through, staring at the heap of M&M's I'd poured into his hand. "I had you pegged as a kale chip and raw almonds kind of girl."

I popped a couple into my mouth. "Maybe you should stop making assumptions about me since you have yet to get one right."

Kel pressed into the fence, staring at me. "Maybe I will." His eyes held mine for a few more seconds before jogging onto the field to warm up. He threw all the M&M's into his mouth at once. "Beats the hell out of kale!"

Grinning, I headed over to my dry patch of bleacher, ripping into my licorice rope. It became hard to concentrate on the game without fixating on him. No matter how hard I tried to pretend I was watching the game, I was certain it was blindingly clear that I was only paying attention to number thirty-three.

When it was Kel's turn to bat, he made it a point to grin

over at me as he headed toward the plate. A few spectators turned around to see who he was looking at.

"Where?" He paused at the fence, calling out to me.

More heads turned.

"What?" I mouthed.

"Where should I hit it?" he clarified, his smile holding.

I lifted my finger, stabbing it toward the back of the field. "Out of the park."

Kel's head shook as a few muffled chuckles circulated the bleachers. "Specifically out where?"

My finger moved left as I batted my eyes. "How about left field, like Barry Bonds when he hit his seven hundred sixty-second home run?"

Kel tapped the end of his bat against the fence, blinking like he didn't recognize me.

"Told you I liked baseball."

"You said you *liked* baseball. Not that you could pop off stats like some old-school sports announcer." Kel lifted his chin as he continued toward the plate. "I'm impressed, Red."

"Now it's your turn to impress me." I gave him a wide smile. "Swing for the fences, thirty-three."

Kel gave a half salute before squatting into position, kind of crowding the plate as he lifted the bat. Megan's reminder to snap a picture of him jumped to mind, but that was *Not. Happening.*

The first pitch thrown was so high and outside, the catcher barely caught it. The ump behind the plate called a ball. Ya think?

Kel shuffled back, took a couple of practice swings, then stepped up to the plate again. The dugout went quiet. No one was cheering his name or number, but everyone was watching number thirty-three, holding their breath like I was.

The second pitch moved so fast it was a blur, and then there was a sharp crack. Everyone in the stands rose, along with Riverview High's team in the dugout. Kel dropped his bat and charged first base as the ball kept sailing into the field. *Left* field. Exactly where I'd pointed.

Along with being a legitimate badass, Kel Remington possessed athletic superpowers. We truly couldn't have been more different. I may have loved baseball, but that didn't mean I could play it. Certainly not like that.

The ball landed over the fence, and without delay the umpire raised his hand to the sky, twirling his finger signaling a home run. It made the skin on my arms rise just like it had when Nick took me to my first pro game. The wave of affection toward Nick caught me off guard, but I turned my focus back to the game. Home run. The team was cheering now as a couple of other guys jogged the bases toward home plate as well. Kel, though? He was still sprinting. Hauling ass was a better description of it. By the time he was rushing toward home, he'd almost caught up to the guy who'd been on second when Kel had gone up to bat.

I stood with the rest of the crowd, clapping my hands and cheering wildly.

Three runs were added to Riverview High's score after Kel crossed home plate. Sliding off the big plastic helmet on his head, he started for the dugout. He wasn't parading like the other guys or pumping his fist in the air. He just moved like he was gliding between classes. No big deal. As he passed my part of the fence, he stalled for a moment.

"That about the right spot?" His smile, the way his sweaty hair stuck to his forehead, the rushed breath coming from his lips . . . crap. It only made me more attracted to him.

"You were a couple of feet off, actually."

He snorted, calling my bluff.

The crowd was having fun listening in on our commentary, like we were part of the entertainment.

As the game continued, I couldn't help noticing the way Kel and his team interacted. It wasn't like they singled him out or he separated himself from them, but there was a careful distance. An unspoken agreement. They exchanged the occasional word or two with him, Kel the same, but he wasn't part of the rest of it. The other players would cluster up, chatting and laughing in between innings. There was an ease between all of them that didn't translate to Kel.

They weren't going out of their way to exclude him—it was simpler than that. They were all more alike than different, and Kel . . . he was his own entity.

"We've taken a vote and it's unanimous." From nowhere, Madeline and Allison popped up beside me, wedging themselves onto the bleacher. "You're coming to every baseball game. Home *and* away."

I scooted over to make space. "I wasn't planning on this becoming a regular thing."

"It's about to become real regular," Allison said as she draped an old plaid blanket over the three of our laps. "Because Kel Remington has hit a home run every time he's been up to bat. You're like his good luck charm."

Eager to get off the Kel topic, I asked, "Did you guys just get here or something? The game's almost done."

"Nah. We were sitting on the other team's side for the beginning. We know some people who go to Parkview."

I shook my licorice rope at them. "You two are in a leadership class and were sitting on enemy sidelines? That's messed up."

Madeline rolled her eyes. "We were cheering both teams, so you could say we're bipartisan. Setting an example on how to be good sports."

Allison beamed smugly. "So . . ." Just the way she said it had me bracing. "What is going on with you and Kel Remington?"

"What do you mean?" The innocent face I put on didn't fool her.

"Please don't make me clarify that. It would be a waste of both of our time." Allison nudged me as Kel and his team were taking the field. He glanced over at me as he jogged, like he was checking to see if I was still there. "Still going to try and deny it?"

I slumped in my seat. "Ugh. I don't know. We hang out."

"Hang out?" Allison blinked at me. "With Kel Remington?"

"Yes." When she continued staring at me, I added, "Why is that so hard to believe?"

"Because nobody is friends with Kel. People respect him. They know him. They notice him. But nobody is *friends* with him."

Exhaling, I pointed at the field, where he was throwing a ball with a few players. "He's friends with people."

"He's a member of the team, yeah, but I know for a fact he's never shown his face at any of the parties."

"I'm sure he has other friends besides me."

Allison blinked at me. "Yeah, sure."

"Come on. You've seen the way the halls part when he moves through them," I said. "That's not how loners with zero friends are treated in high school."

"No, but that's how people act when something dangerous comes close." Allison blinked at Madeline, like she was waiting for backup, but Madeline kept chewing on her lip.

"Really? Kel?" I laughed, even though I didn't totally disagree with her.

"Seriously, Quinn. The way people act around him, tiptoeing around him, a person doesn't make friends with that unless they want to wind up . . ."

When her voice trailed off, I turned to face her. "What?" My eyes lifted. "Dead?"

She gave a little shrug. "Metaphorically speaking?"

I stared at the field, between second and third base. "He isn't like that."

"How do you know?"

All evidence that Kel could have been a threat jumped to mind: the bruises, his reputation, Nick wanting me to stay away from him, where he lived, it all came rushing to my mind. Then I took a good look at him, not just what he wanted people to see, but what he didn't want them to.

"I know" was all I answered.

Allison was about to say something else when her phone rang. She checked the screen and gave an exasperated sigh. "It's my mom. I promised I'd watch my little brothers tonight so she and Dad could go to dinner."

When she stood up, Madeline rose with her. "I've got

to bail too, but I think it's safe to say I know who's going to win."

"Bye. Thanks for sharing the blanket." I exhaled as they glided off the bleacher, feeling like I was off the hook. Madeline and Allison waved as they jogged toward the parking lot. It was nice to have someone to check up on me—even if I could've done without the invasive questions.

"Still like baseball, then?"

I jolted, for real jolted, when I heard his voice. Nick had somehow crept up beside me and was watching the game like he'd been there the whole time. "Maybe we can catch a Mariners game sometime."

Once I'd semi-recovered, I found myself feeling strangely sentimental. Something that almost resembled excitement at the thought of attending a Mariners game with the man I didn't want to be in the same room as not too long ago. "Oh. Sure."

After that, he was quiet. A couple of rings of keys hung from one of his belt loops, the hollows beneath his eyes black from what I guessed was lack of sleep thanks to shuffling our rooms around yesterday.

"I haven't had a chance to . . . I mean I wanted to . . ." Words turned to glue in my mouth, impossible to articulate. Taking a breath, I tried again. "Thank you for the bedroom swap. You didn't have to—"

Nick's head shook. "A fifteen-year-old girl should have her own space. One she can close, lock, or slam a door to."

My hands twisted in my lap, waiting for him to bring up the fact I'd fled the apartment when we'd last seen each other. It never came up, though. Instead, Nick stood there, watching half an inning with me and the rest of the spectators.

As Riverview High left the field, Kel scanned the crowd and found me watching him. He winked. And of course my father was two feet away when he did.

Kel didn't see Nick.

Nick didn't miss Kel.

"Maybe it's not baseball you're into after all." Nick scanned between Kel and me, his tone sharp enough to give away what he thought about the two of us.

"He's just a friend," I said, staring at the field because I was too scared to glance over at Nick and have him see what I was trying to hide from him, everyone else, and most especially, myself.

Nick exhaled. "And I'm just your dad."

No one will ever be your everything. You be your own everything first. Then find someone special who feels the same way.

"I can pick you up at your place around twelve-thirty on Saturday if that works." Kel looked up from his math homework Wednesday night.

I'd been zoning out, specifically on the way his jaw tensed whenever he was working on a difficult problem. Clearing my throat, I dropped my gaze to his assignment, like that's where all my attention had been.

"Are you sure you still want to do that? It's a bunch of people you don't know. A town the size of a marble compared to here. Then there's the two-hundred-fifty-mile round-trip drive." I kept my eyes on his homework because I'd had an increasingly difficult time looking at him the past few days without having some kind of inappropriate reaction. Like blushing. Or light-headedness. Or a quickening pulse.

"I'm sure," he said, copying down the next math problem. "For the hundredth time," he added under his breath.

"Your mom doesn't mind?"

His pencil stopped moving. "She doesn't mind," he said, back to writing down the problem.

My fingers rolled along the table. Something was off. He was acting different around me. He kept everything he said to a minimum and would barely look at me. Maybe it was something I'd said or done, or maybe it was nothing to do with me at all, but it was driving me nuts.

"How was baseball practice?" I asked as he kept working.

"Good."

"You guys have an away game tomorrow, right?"

He erased what he'd just written down. "Yeah."

My fingers kept drumming. We were down to one-word responses now. This wasn't the progress I was hoping to make.

Since Kel appeared to have developed the laser focus of a hawk, I decided to try a different approach. "Yeah, so I guess a bunch of senior guys are having this big party Friday night. They're only inviting the underclassman girls. I'll probably go. They have a hot tub, and Luke has been looking pretty cute lately." I took a breath, slumping in my seat when he gave a mumble of acknowledgment, still concentrating on that damn math assignment.

My hands pounded down on the table. "Kel!"

The pencil fell from his hands as he jumped from his seat like we were under attack. "What?"

I rose from my chair, slanting across the table and planting my hands on the surface. "I was getting tired of being ignored," I said, feeling my heart begin to hum faster with his eyes on me. "Just looking for a way to get your attention."

Kel didn't blink as he moved closer, until he was pressed against the edge of the table. Leaning forward like I was, he scooted his math book and homework aside and planted his hands on the table in front of mine.

Except they didn't stay there. One of his hands slipped closer, his fingers splitting between mine before knotting around them. My heart was pounding so hard, I was convinced that if I peeked down at my chest, I would see it bouncing against my rib cage.

His face moved closer, until I could smell the minty freshness on his breath from the gum he'd been chewing. His fingers tightened, before his hand curled mine up into his fist. So gentle, it was like he was holding a butterfly in his palm. One dark brow carved into his forehead. "Okay, Red. You've got my attention."

He was only holding my hand, a linoleum-top table separating us, but my body was tingling like every part of him was touching every piece of me.

"So?" Kel's voice was lower than normal, throatier. "Now that you have it, what are you going to do with it?"

When his eyes dropped to my mouth, I figured he had the general idea. Right as I was about to lean that last few inches closer, the entire library exploded with light.

"A couple of kids can't study very well in the dark." Nick was stationed beside the wall where a panel of light switches was, gaping between Kel and me like he'd stumbled on a crime scene.

I leaned away. Kel let my hand go, but not before Nick

noticed. "Conserving electricity," I said, waving up at the row of lights we'd had on. "Don't need to flood the whole library with light when there's only two of us."

Nick's attention was on Kel. I was pretty sure there was a serious warning in that glare he gave him, but I didn't speak male bravado. I'd expected Kel to blow it off or roll his eyes, but instead, he dropped his gaze in surrender.

"That's exactly the reason this whole room should be, and will remain, lit up." Nick flicked on the last switch—the one illuminating the offices behind the checkout area. Talk about overkill. "I'll be back in half an hour, Quinn. Try to have things wrapped up by then."

He was gone before I could say anything, the jingle of his key rings fading into the hallway. My blood was doing that boil thing again, begging for some kind of release, but I had no idea how to vent it.

"Hey, it's only because he cares about you." Kel's voice was calm as he gathered up his stuff.

"Huh?" I was still too upset to think straight.

"If he didn't care, he wouldn't say anything." Kel threw his bag on, glancing at me like he was waiting for me to do the same. "Don't be mad at him for giving a shit."

"Oh, great. The one person who should be on my side on this is crossing enemy lines."

One corner of Kel's mouth twitched as I began to toss books into my bag. "Hey, if I had a daughter who was spending time with a guy like me, I'd go all psycho dad on his ass too."

"No you wouldn't." I flung my bag on and scooted the chair under the table.

Kel seemed to be amused by my mini bout of rage. "You know I would."

I groaned. "You're not the bad guy."

Kel met me at the end of the table. "I'm not the good guy either."

"You know, you keep saying that, but it hasn't yet scared me away." We moved together toward the exit.

"I keep trying." He grinned over at me, but his eyes weren't in it.

When we made it to the door, I reached for his hand. This time it was my fingers that knotted through his. "Stop trying."

Kel was quiet, staring at where our hands were connected. When he exhaled, it was almost like a weight had evaporated. "Okay," he breathed. "I'll stop."

Flipping off the lights behind us, I let him guide me into the darkness.

Laugh at yourself. No really.

Like right now.

Isn't everything instantly better?

I was going home. My mood was downright giddy—on the annoying spectrum of that emotion. Kel had done a good job of putting up with it the past couple of hours, despite him usually being anti-glee.

"It was so cool of your mom to let us borrow her truck," I said for the fifth or sixth time so far. "Make sure to tell her thank you."

Kel nodded, appearing ever so serious behind the steering wheel of the old pick-up. "Will do."

"It's weird seeing you drive." I twisted in my seat, angling toward him.

"Weird?" he echoed. "It's kind of a rite of passage for most kids when they turn sixteen."

"Yeah. I better get on that. Sixteen's right around the corner." I sipped the last melted drink of my blue raspberry ice.

"Can't wait to earn your freedom?"

My head turned toward the window, taking in the familiar landscape whizzing by. "Something like that."

The emancipation paperwork tucked away in my room jumped to mind. I was surprised to realize I hadn't given it much thought lately. Things were going smoother with Nick. Although I still found myself wondering why Mom chose him over the list of others who were, honestly, more qualified to take me on, I had to admit I felt almost thankful she had. We were getting the chance at a new start. I'd even cleared my all-day adventure with him . . . though I might have forgotten to mention the part about Kel. And the part about going to Leavenworth.

"So this is home?" Kel said, checking through the windshield at the mountains and blue sky as if we'd arrived on a different planet.

I had to roll down the window to let in the smell. Even though it was cool, the mountains patched in snow, I could sense spring in the air. It had become a yearly tradition with Mom and me. Waiting for the smell of spring. It hadn't arrived, but it wasn't too far off either.

"Where do you want to go first?" Kel asked as we passed the Leavenworth sign greeting visitors. "Did you want to go see your mom?" And with that I remembered this homecoming wouldn't be all smiles and fun. A weight settled inside my stomach. The last time I'd been here was when we'd buried her. As much as I missed her, I still wasn't ready to revisit that cemetery. I wasn't sure if I ever would be.

Mom was gone. What was left of her in that place wasn't the person I'd loved.

My head shook as I worked to swallow the lump in my throat. "Why don't we park downtown so I can give you the unofficial city tour? I promise it will be quick." I tried a smile, but it felt wrong. Why didn't I want to visit my mom's grave? What was I so scared would be waiting there?

"As long as I'm not required to wear lederhosen for the tour, I'm down with that plan." Kel stopped to let a family go through the crosswalk, peeking through the windows at the city up ahead.

"My mom bribed me into one of the Bavarian outfits when I was five for a maypole dance. Never again."

Kel laughed as I pointed him down a couple of streets to find parking. March was a quieter month for the town, winter and summer bringing droves of tourists who loved the festive activities Leavenworth provided. Still, it was a Saturday, so it took a few turns before we could find a place to park on the street.

"Wow. This place really embraces the German village thing," Kel said, taking in the buildings in front of us.

"Come on. I'll buy you a brat and a salted pretzel. Before we get you fit for those lederhosen." I scrambled out of the truck before he could reply.

As soon as my feet touched the sidewalk on Front Street, I sighed. I was home. The air, the sounds, the bustle of people moving in and out of shops; I could have cried.

"What kind of music is that?" Kel asked as he came around the truck.

"Polka," I asserted.

"And the smell?"

"Sauerkraut. And beer," I added as we passed one of the popular beer gardens in town.

My walking tour of town didn't take long since the bulk of downtown was about six blocks long and two blocks wide. He asked a few questions, but mostly he observed. We ran into a few of the shop owners and employees I knew, exchanging quick hellos and hugs, but no one mentioned my mom. No one could bear to bring up the move, Nick, or the new life I'd essentially gotten no say in.

"Being here, seeing this place, I get it now," Kel finally said after a while.

"You get what now?" My pace slowed as the building ahead of us came into view.

"You."

"Me?"

"Only a person who grew up in a place like this could see the good in anything. Or anyone."

I shot a look of fake shock at him. "Are you insulting my beloved hometown?"

Kel lifted his hands and scooted to the side. "Not at all. Just taking it in." His eyes roamed the scene in front of us. "Weird music, strange smells, a mess of tourists, all in a small, compact space, and you're grinning like a kid at the entrance to Disneyland."

I bent over to pick up a water bottle someone had dropped on the sidewalk. "It's home. Doesn't everyone love where they come from?"

Kel followed me to the closest garbage can. "No," he said. "Not everyone."

As we started to pass a yellow building, my pace picked up and my head focused straight ahead.

"Hello, speed demon. Why the sudden race after the stroll down memory lane?"

"Because not all memories need to be dwelled upon. Some you should rush by as fast as possible." I didn't check inside the restaurant, knowing there'd be a mess of familiar faces. I'd spent plenty of time studying at corner tables while Mom finished a late shift, and her coworkers had become like family in a lot of ways. I'd forgotten that some pieces of home would be painful.

Kel kept up with my quickened pace, not saying a thing. I was relieved he didn't. Thankful he understood.

We turned down the next road to make one more stop before heading to the party. "Does your mom come to your baseball games very often?" I still hadn't seen Kel's mom. If it wasn't for the way he talked about her, I could have believed she was a ghost.

"No. She doesn't."

I paused to pick my words carefully. The topics of Kel's mom and home life were like tiptoeing through a minefield— I trod carefully.

"Is she feeling better?" I asked, figuring this fell in the safe category, especially since he'd said she was sick when I'd suggested swinging by his place for tutoring after his game this past week.

Kel kicked at a pebble on the sidewalk. "About the same."

Another pause to construct the right words. "Maybe I could make some soup and bring it by tomorrow? I make a mean bean and ham soup."

Kel's head started shaking only a few words in. "No, it's okay. She doesn't like visitors. But thanks," he added, touching his shoulder to mine. "I bet you do make a killer soup, though."

As we silently got into Kel's truck and began the short drive to Megan's house, I couldn't help wondering what he was trying to keep hidden. For all his talk of honesty, he was skilled in the art of keeping secrets.

"Ready to head into a party full of strangers?" I asked when I pointed to the house up ahead.

Kel gave a low whistle when he pulled into the driveway as he appraised Megan's family's place. They lived on a pretty patch of land a mile up Ski Hill Drive, their house built in the style of a grand chalet one would expect to find in the Alps. Or the Alps of Washington in this case. "They know I'm coming, right?" he asked.

"Yep," I said. I had told Meg I was bringing someone. But like Nick, she may also have missed the memo that this someone was a guy.

Kel met me around the truck, taking my purse to ease the load I was juggling in my arms. "Can't seem so tough when you're carrying a purse in the shape of a cat, can you?"

In response, he put the strap over his shoulder. "Better?"

"*So* tough." I laughed.

A couple of balloon bouquets were framing the doorway; the sound of music and laughter came from inside. I'd known most of the people since kindergarten—I'd been *dying* to see them for weeks—but my palms began to sweat as I rang the bell. Part of that was bringing Kel, and part of it was being at my first get-together like this since Mom had died. I didn't want things to be awkward, or want everyone to treat me like I was fragile and saying the wrong thing would shatter me. I wanted normal. To pretend like everything was the same.

The sound of footsteps bounding toward the door echoed inside. "COMING!!!"

When Meg threw open the door, I grinned. She had a cockeyed party hat settled on her corkscrew blond hair, confetti tangled in bouncy curls. When she saw me, Meg threw her hands to her chest, batting her baby blues like the drama club kid she was. "Oh my goodness, my little girl's come home at last!" Without warning, she launched herself at me. "Don't you stay away so long, you hear? My delicate sensibilities can't bear it."

"Missed you too, Meg," I breathed once she eased up on her death grip enough for my lungs to regain function.

Suddenly, she seemed to notice there was a rather hard-to-ignore someone beside me. She peeled herself off me, combing at her hair as she flashed a pearly white smile in Kel's direction. "And pray, do tell, who is this strapping young lad who's escorted you to the soiree this fine eve?"

"Why don't you come out of character, Miss O'Hara, and stop scaring us, so I can introduce you to the kindly gentleman." I winked at Kel as I said it. He just shook his head.

"Megan, meet Kel." I waved between the two of them. "Kel, meet Megan. She's slightly imbalanced," I whispered to him.

Meg pinched me. "So this is what happens when a girl moves to the Seattle area," she said, blinking at Kel like he'd just descended from the heavens or something. "Want a roommate?" she asked me, dead serious.

"I would gladly take you over my current one," I said as Meg led us inside the house.

"Speaking of the current roommate . . ." Meg stopped just before the living room. "Are things getting any better with him?"

"Mildly. But things will be *much* better when I can move out," I answered, dropping Raven's present off on the table overflowing with gifts. "But I don't want to talk about any of that today. I just want to have fun."

Meg grabbed something from the table, lifting it above my head ceremoniously. "Fun awaits you, fair maiden," she sang, snapping a party hat on my head.

When she moved to grab another one, Kel dodged her reach. "I don't do party hats."

I had to cover my mouth when the picture of him wearing one popped to mind.

Meg's eyes dropped to his side. "No, of course not. Kitty purses are more your thing."

Like he'd just remembered it was there, Kel slipped it from his shoulder and held it for me to take now that my hands were free.

"It looks good on you," I teased, taking it.

"*Better* on you, though."

Meg was watching the two of us carefully. Before she could start with the questions, I herded us into the living room. Streamers and balloons were strung over anything that was stationary, the lights dim so the spinning disco ball could splash silver squares across the walls as it spun. There were a couple dozen people there, and I recognized them all.

Something warm and light filled me up as I took in the

scene. Right before I realized everyone was now staring at us, eyes pinging between Kel and me.

"Everyone, this is Kel," I announced to the room. "Kel, this is Everyone."

I nudged Meg, who acted quickly. "I thought this was a party." She cupped her hands over her mouth and roared, "So let's party!"

A cheer traveled through the room as people got back to whatever they'd been doing before inspecting the stranger at my side.

"Where's Raven?" I asked Meg, squinting at the crowd to find her. With the lack of light and all the bodies bouncing around, I couldn't tell the difference between Dina and David.

"Raven's right here!" a familiar voice rang out from behind.

Before I had a chance to turn around, Raven had pounced on me, her tiny dancer arms squeezing me like she should have tried out for the football team instead of the dance team. When she noticed Kel beside me, she mouthed over at me, "Day-um."

Thankfully, the darkness hid the color flooding my face.

"Hey, I'm Raven." She stuck her hand toward Kel, like his six foot something didn't intimate her five foot nothing in the slightest.

"Happy birthday." He shook her hand. "I'm Kel."

"I should let you know, Kel, that Quinn is my girl. We've been through a lot together and I would do anything for this chica." Raven's arm slung over my shoulders as she stared Kel straight on. "You hurt her—I'll break you."

"Raven," I hissed, more color seeping into my already red face.

Once Kel finished fighting a smile, his expression got serious. "If I hurt Quinn, I'll save you the trouble and break myself."

Raven's head angled, studying him like he was a grand jeté she was attempting to master. "I approve. You can continue dating my dear beloved friend."

Neither of us brought up the fact that we weren't technically dating.

"Help yourself to pizza, soda, cake, whatever you want. You know your way around the kitchen," Meg said, moving toward the door, where someone had rung the bell. "But don't think you're going to bail before you and I have a little heart-to-heart, mano a mano." Meg twirled her finger at me.

I crossed my heart in answer, which seemed to satisfy her.

Raven had melted back into the party, dancing as only a girl who truly didn't care a crap what people thought could.

"Well," I said to Kel, impressed that he didn't appear the least bit intimidated by any of this. "What do you want to do?"

His head turned, the lights refracted around the room catching in his eyes. "Whatever you want to do."

"Follow me," I said, leading the way into the crowd.

It took forever to make our way through everyone, because no one was happy with a quick hi and bye. They all wanted to chat about the latest happenings. Plus they all had their questions for Kel, who fielded them like a champ.

At first, you could tell people couldn't quite decide what to make of the two of us, especially since the most rebellious thing I'd done growing up was sneak a bottle of Mom's kirsch from the top cupboard. My rebellion didn't last long, though. I tried a sip, hated it, and then promptly dumped half of it down the drain to see if she'd realize any was missing, and I was the likely culprit. Mom never noticed.

"I'm thirsty," I shouted over at him after making the rounds. "And hot." The temperature, along with the music volume, had dialed up a hundred notches.

"I'll get you something," Kel leaned in so he didn't have to shout. That mixture of soap, sweat, and boy clouded my senses. "Why don't you go cool down?" He motioned at the sliding glass doors behind me that led into the back.

Nodding, I thanked him and headed out. This wasn't the party to wear a long-sleeved dress and sweater tights to. I should have known that from having attended dozens of parties Meg had hosted, but apparently time away had made me forget.

As soon as I opened the door, a rush of cool air washed over me. I wandered across the deck, waving at a couple huddled around the gas fireplace.

I kept walking to give them privacy until finally the party noise had grown to a faint din behind me.

"Trying to hide from me way out here in the dark?" The sound of Kel moving through the yard came from behind me.

"I thought you were able to see in the dark."

Kel made a grunt of acknowledgment. "We evolved types do possess that ability."

He held up a plastic cup filled with something clear and bubbling. Sprite. He'd gotten it right, without having to ask.

His own cup was filled with something dark and fizzy.

We stood there, drinking and staring down at the little town I'd grown up in, lights twinkling in the distance.

"You know what I've realized after all the times I've moved in my life?" Kel's arm touched mine, his head falling back. "That no matter where you wind up, the sky pretty much always looks the same."

My head fell back with his, taking in the stars splashed against the black canvas. I studied them for a minute. Then another. "You're right," I said, my hand somehow finding its way into his. "It's always there."

At the same time, each of us stared over at the other. "The other day, when we were in the library, we were talking about us—" When Kel's head began to shake, I kept going. "I need to know what this is, Kel. I don't deal well with the undefined."

His jaw moved as I stepped closer. "What do you need defined, Quinn?"

"I think you know," I whispered.

"And I think you already know the answer to that."

I set down my cup and slowly placed my hand on his chest. It was moving fast, the beat of his heart pushing into my palm. "I need to hear you say it."

His eyes closed, his brows pinching together like my touch was physically hurting him.

"You're wincing." I swallowed as my gaze wandered his face.

"Not because you're touching me." Kel's voice was strained as he forced his eyes back open. "But because I'm so damn close to touching you."

My heart started beating so hard, I could feel it ringing in my ears. "It's okay, Kel." I erased the last bit of space keeping us apart. Now we were touching. I felt a tremor spill down his spine.

"It's not okay." His hand covering mine skimmed down to my wrist, winding around it. "Someone like me wanting someone like you . . ." He shook his head. "It's not okay."

"Why isn't it?" My voice echoed around us, not quite like his.

"It's selfish." He stared at me like he didn't understand why he had to explain this to me. "You're on one level, and I'm on another."

Heat pumped through my veins, part from anger, part from want. "I'm here." My voice shook as my hand pressed into his chest. "And you're here. That's all I care about."

"It isn't so simple."

"It is. I promise you it is that simple." My hand moved up, cupping into the bend of his neck. His skin was hot, nearly scalding to the touch. My eyes dropped to his mouth as my body pressed nearer. "Kel . . ."

His hand dropped to my shoulder, holding me at a distance. "I can't kiss you, Quinn."

"Why not?"

A breath spilled past his lips. "Because I like you too much."

My face drew up.

"That makes zero sense."

"In my world, it makes all the sense," he replied.

My fingers slipped around his neck farther, not making this easy for him. "Then live in a different one for a while."

"Like where?"

"Mine." My voice pierced the night, spreading around us. "Try living in mine."

Kel's body tensed somehow even more. "I'm afraid I'll destroy it if you let me in."

My thumb brushed up the line of his jaw. "I'm not afraid of you, Kel Remington."

A tremble rocked through him. "You should be."

I lifted an eyebrow. "You should be afraid of me."

"I am. Terrified."

He wasn't teasing; he was serious. "Of what?"

Kel's arm at my shoulder began to relax. "Everything." Yet even as he said it, his hand skimmed around my back, drawing me to him; his other hand dropped from my neck to my waist.

His head lowered, our eyes meeting right before his mouth touched mine. A jolt of energy rushed through me, warm and overwhelming. At first, his lips rested against my own, still and sweet.

Popping up onto my tiptoes, I pressed my lips harder to his, causing a deep rumble to echo in his chest. His arm looped farther around me as all the tension seemed to drain from him at once.

And then I was kissing Kel Remington. *Really* kissing him.

It was everything I'd hoped my first kiss would be and nothing that I could have prepared myself for. I didn't know lips touching lips could affect so many other parts of the body. Like the way my lungs seemed to have collapsed or the way my heart felt like it was trying to take off or the way my muscles felt solid and liquid all at the same time.

His fingers curled into me at my back, like he was trying to pull me even tighter to him, but I couldn't get any closer without becoming a part of him. My head was spinning by the time he pulled away. His dark eyes opened into mine, a gleam in them I'd never seen before. They were light, happy, but there was something lurking behind all that too, something almost dangerous.

I could still taste him on my lips; I could practically feel him against them, like he'd left his imprint behind.

"You kissed me," I breathed, smiling up at him.

His lips were parted, a rushed breath pulling through them. I'd never seen him so conflicted, like he'd been forcing himself to hold back at the same time he'd finally given in.

"Sorry," he said at last, a smile playing at the corner of his mouth.

My head shook as I lifted my other hand to his neck. "Finally."

Give second chances freely.

Third ones scarcely.

We'd stayed later than we planned, but neither of us was eager to get back to the reality Renton would mean. It was eleven by the time we finally forced ourselves to leave the party, which was still in full swing, promising everyone we'd make another visit soon. My friends liked Kel. Kel liked them. It was too good to be true.

That was the theme of the whole night. Getting to come home, spend an evening with my best friends, breaking through the wall Kel had kept between us, getting to kiss him . . . these were the kinds of days that were hard to beat.

I think we both felt the heaviness of reality as we turned off the interstate to take our exit. But I was glad to see Kel's hand still twisted through mine.

"Thanks again for driving me all the way home," I said. "This whole day. It was exactly what I needed."

Kel smiled at the windshield. "Anytime."

I found myself watching him more than usual, feeling like it was acceptable now that we'd crossed that physical line. Everything about him seemed relaxed, like someone had pulled the plug that held the tension he seemed to carry with him at all times.

But there was something in his eyes that was different, too. Worry, perhaps. It seemed an odd thing for someone like him to harbor, but I knew Kel had his reasons.

"Are you *still* terrified of me?" I teased as he made the last turn toward my apartment.

"Even more now." He peered over at me from the corner of his eye.

"More?" I sat up in my seat. "Why?"

He didn't answer my question. Or maybe he did, but I failed to read the message on his face. Either way, our time was up. The truck had just braked to a stop in front of the apartment building.

"You're home," he said, peering through the windows, checking to make sure it was safe for me to walk the whole twenty feet to the entrance.

"I'm here," I corrected him, reaching for the handle, my hand pausing on it. I didn't want to leave. I didn't want this night to end. I wondered whether, if I asked him to pull away and just keep driving, he would. Something told me I could ask him just about anything, and if Kel could, he'd do it. But I also knew I shouldn't abuse that power.

My hand would not open the door. It felt incapable.

"So . . . you and me . . ." I swallowed, not sure how to sum up what Kel and I were. "We're good now?"

Kel finished checking through the windows, then angled in his seat toward me. His hand lifted to my cheek, his fingers brushing against my skin so carefully I barely felt them. "We're good."

I leaned across my seat toward him.

"I thought you were leaving." Kel's face dropped toward mine, his eyes falling to my mouth.

"So did I."

My lips brushed his just as the passenger door flew open, my hand still attached to the handle. As I was spilling from my seat, Kel's arm roped around me, catching me before I toppled outside.

Kel glared into the night, his expression lethal. It changed the moment he realized who it was standing outside.

"It's time to say good night, Quinn." I heard him before I saw him.

When I checked over my shoulder, I found Nick, his jaw set and his eyes wild. "I was just saying bye."

Nick moved aside, waving me out. "Now, Quinn."

My whole face burned when I realized Nick had witnessed my almost-kiss with Kel.

I had to bite my lip to keep from talking back to Nick when everything inside me was dying to. That could wait for later. There was no reason to drag Kel into the Nick-and-Quinn showdown. "Good night, Kel."

His hand found mine as I was sliding away. I didn't miss the fire that lit in Nick's eyes when he saw that. "Are you all right?" Kel asked me.

I was just about to answer when Nick marched in front of me. "She will be all right as long as you stay the hell away from her, you hear me?"

I blinked, not sure if this was really happening.

"You have no right—*none*—to think you have anything to offer this girl." Nick's voice shook as he kept going while I stood there, frozen from shock and denial. "I want you to put this truck in drive, pull away, and *stay* away."

I couldn't see Kel with Nick stationed in front of me. I had no idea if he was about to lose his cool or if he was giving Nick the same kind of amused smirk I'd seen aimed my way so many times.

"I care about her." Kel's voice sounded muffled. "I'd never do anything to hurt her."

Nick snorted, shaking his head. "You and I both know that there's only one way you can keep that promise to me. By staying away from her."

"Nick, stop." My body came back to life, trying to wedge itself between him and Kel. I couldn't budge him.

A moment later, Nick slammed the door closed, and then Kel pulled away. As he drove off, I could finally see him through the rear window. He didn't look back like I thought he would. I don't think he even checked the mirror. He left. Just like Nick told him to do.

"You're to stay away from that boy, you hear me, Quinn?" Nick spun around once Kel's truck had disappeared down the street.

"You're screaming! Of course I hear you!" I shouted, reality soaking in.

"That boy is no good for you." Nick's arm thrust down the street, his finger pointing at where Kel had disappeared.

Sadness had an odd way of masking itself as anger. I was familiar with its deception, but I gave myself over to it anyway. "You're one to talk! Why can't you just leave me alone like you did before Mom died!"

The emotion leached from Nick's face instantly, all the tension draining from him at the same time. In the time it took me to blink, he'd transformed into a being who seemed more dead than alive.

My stomach turned when I witnessed the power of my words. Crossing my arms, I whisked past him toward the apartment. "You don't get to tell me who I can and can't have in my life."

I was almost to the entrance when his voice echoed from behind me. "It's only because I care, Quinn."

I pulled the door open and kept moving. "Caring isn't enough."

When Monday morning finally came around, I bolted from bed as soon as my alarm went off. Nick could have been gone for the day or he could have still been asleep inside his curtain room. I didn't stick around to see.

I'd slipped into the same dress and tights I'd worn Saturday night, in some foolish hope that the same outfit would re-create the same feeling. It was yet another rainy day, so I had to cinch up my raincoat over my dress, but once I'd escaped, I made record time to the high school.

In my rush, I'd gotten there early, so I stationed myself on the south side of the school, where I'd have a view of Kel as he made his way in. There was no way I could wait until lunchtime to talk to him.

The minutes kept ticking by, the rain plunking against my raincoat. He should be coming any second now. Any second.

I was still repeating that after the first-period bell rang. Where was he? My shoulders slumped into the brick wall behind me as I tried to decide what to do now. Wait a few minutes in hopes he was just running late? Risk going to his place to make sure he was okay? Or had he had an early-morning baseball practice and already been at school when I'd arrived?

The answer to my questions came a minute later in the form of a tall, dark shadow striding down the sidewalk. My heart quickened seeing him, even from a hundred yards away. His eyes were aimed at the pavement, so he didn't see me waiting. He was walking kind of funny, favoring his right side.

"Kel!" I called when he kept moving toward the entrance.

He hadn't seen me, it was clear from the surprise on his face. He smiled automatically, but his smile faded away quickly. By the time he was taking the last few steps toward me, the flat expression he typically wore was back in place.

"What is it, Quinn?" His stare stayed turned down.

My chest throbbed, knowing the wall had been rebuilt. Feeling it rising between us. "Can we talk?"

Kel checked around at the quiet parking lot and sidewalks. "What are you doing? First period already started."

"Exactly. So why aren't you in class?"

He didn't answer my question. Instead, his hand dropped

to my elbow and he led me around the side of the building. "Quinn, we can talk about this later."

"I don't want to talk later." I shrugged free from his hold, planting my feet. "I want to talk now. I've been waiting all weekend to talk."

"Later. I promise." He rolled his neck, taking a breath. "Right now, let's get you to class. I don't need to confirm your dad's predictions."

I moved my arm when he reached for it again. I was not going to be herded. I was not going to be soothed. "You're not actually thinking about staying away from me because he told you to, are you?" I asked. "Kel?"

He managed to steer me under an overhang so the rain couldn't get me, but it was only big enough for one of us. He stayed in front, taking on the rain like he barely noticed it. "Maybe."

My fingers curled into my palms, nails digging into flesh. "Maybe *not*."

Kel's hand lifted, combing a loose chunk of my hair back inside my raincoat's hood. "I don't want to hurt you. But it's pretty much a guarantee I will."

"No. It's not."

"No? If I'm such a great influence, why are you here waiting for me, skipping class? How is this in any way beneficial to you?"

My mouth opened, but no words came. "I just . . . missed you." As my hands went to slip around his sides, he flinched at my touch. "What is it?" I asked, his expression suggesting I'd jabbed a knife through his ribs.

"It's nothing." He gritted his teeth, sliding away.

"No, it's something." I moved faster than he was expecting, managing to snag the hem of his sweatshirt in my hand and yank it up before he could stop me.

"Quinn—"

"What the hell." I blinked, not sure what I was seeing. "What happened?" I breathed when the black and blue splotches covering the right side of his torso didn't disappear.

"That's nothing. Forget about it." Kel freed his sweatshirt from me, slipping it down over his stomach.

"Did you get checked? You might have cracked a rib or something." My vision blurred as I appraised him, standing there so tall and unfazed, like he was immune to the pain.

Kel took another step away from me so he was out of arm's reach. "I didn't break a rib."

"How do you know?"

His head turned to the side, like he wasn't going to answer. "Because I know what that feels like, and this doesn't feel like that."

"How do you know what that feels like?"

"Do I really seem like the type of guy who hasn't nursed a few cracked and broken bones in his lifetime?"

"You got in a fight?" I guessed, wondering when? With who? Why?

Kel gave me a pointed look.

"Kel, you can't keep—"

"You can criticize and shout at me later. Right now, you need to get to class." Kel's hand worked around my elbow, managing to get me moving.

"I don't want to yell at you. I want to *talk* to you. About this weekend. About what comes next."

When we were outside the front entrance, he paused, waiting for me to go in first. "We will. I promise," he added when I opened my mouth. "But you're not going to skip class for me, Quinn Winters. That's a nonnegotiable." His head lifted at the doors he was waiting for me to go through. I guess I was supposed to go in first so we weren't seen together or, in Kel's mind, so I wasn't seen coming in late with him.

Rumors could start from that sort of thing. Not that I cared what people wanted to assume or say about the two of us.

"You swear, you promise?" I asked.

Kel kind of smiled. "I swear, I promise."

My teacher was not understanding when it came to first-time offenses in the late department, so I got a tardy, and with it a detention that had to be served in the next week. So much for a flawless attendance record.

When lunch came around, I was the first person into the lunchroom and stationed myself at the door to catch him as soon as he came in. Kel was a no-show, though, so I sat with my usual table and tried my best to seem interested in the pep assembly the leadership class was planning.

By sixth period, I was a mess. Other than this morning, I hadn't seen Kel once. I wasn't sure if that was coincidence or if he was avoiding me, but my gut told me it wasn't by chance.

He didn't show. Mr. Johnson set Kel's quiz from last week down like he was expecting him to arrive eventually, and I couldn't help checking his score. Fifteen out of twenty. Not bad. Actually, it was pretty darn amazing for Kel.

I just wished he was here to see it.

When the end-of-the-day bell rang, I stopped by my locker to grab what I needed for the night and headed straight for the baseball field. He might have chanced skipping sixth to delay our talk, but I doubted he'd skip practice. Baseball was too important to him.

The team wasn't on the field when I got there, but they began to file from the locker room a few minutes later, Kel taking up the tail, still moving like he was in pain. He noticed me camped on the bleachers right away, I could tell, even though he gave no visible indication.

He took straight to the field, warming up with the rest of the team until his coach noticed he was moving funny. I didn't hear what was being said, just saw the coach point to the dugout—twice—before Kel left the field. His gaze stayed on the ground the whole time and remained that way the rest of practice.

I sat there the entire two hours watching. I didn't pull out my homework or a book or distract myself with my phone. I watched him, hoping if I stared long enough, I might finally see whatever it was he was hiding.

When practice wrapped up, Kel rejoined his team and jogged into the locker room, not sparing one look in my direction. I stood, and I followed the same path the team had taken and planted myself outside the locker room. He wasn't going to be able to dodge me this time.

An hour later, long after the rest of the team had gone, finally he marched through the door. He looked at me as if he'd known I'd be waiting.

My arms crossed tighter around myself. "You can't avoid me forever."

"I know." Kel's jaw tensed. "But I was hoping for a little while longer."

"What do you think is going to happen?" I asked.

He adjusted the bag he had hanging from his shoulder, turning his head. "That you'll move on if I keep you waiting long enough."

"Not moving on. No matter how long you stall."

When I wound my arms around him, he flinched.

"Sorry." My arms loosened around his torso as his arm wound around me, drawing me in. As he did so, a breath bled from him, the sound of a person giving in.

"I'm not," he whispered into my hair, holding me like that in silence for a brief forever.

"Your dad," he said, a question and a statement.

"Don't call him that." My head shook against his chest.

"Whatever we call him"—Kel's fingers stopped scrolling my back—"he's not going to want to see us together again."

"Then we'll just have to make sure we don't let him see."

He was quiet for a minute. "You want to go behind his back?"

A pit opened up in my stomach, but it wasn't enough to change my mind. "If that's what it means to be with you."

Kel's chin tucked over my head, relaxing into me in a way I didn't know he was capable of. "I'd do anything for you. Even stay away if that's what you needed."

"That's not what I need. But I do need to know how you got all those bruises."

He took a deep breath. "A fight."

"With who?"

"A guy."

I tipped my head up at him. "Could you be any more vague?"

His foot scuffed at the ground as he pulled me closer. "I can't be any more specific."

*Giving up and moving on are two
very different things.
Never give up. But always move on.*

We'd managed to make it work. For all of three days so far.

Still, it was better than no days. Kel and I were together, but no one could know we were together. At least in "that" way. Especially Nick. He'd been unusually nosy the past few days, but I'd made sure there was nothing for him to sniff out.

Having to be so stealthy meant we'd had to get creative. I'd find folded scraps of paper stuffed into my locker or tucked into my homework, listing a place and a time to meet.

The prop room tucked behind the school's theater became our go-to meeting place. No one was ever there, and even though it was dusty and musky, it was paradise. The one place in the school we didn't have to pretend. The spot he could touch me and I could touch back and no one was around to see or care.

Those stolen moments in the prop closet were what I lived for.

Kel had baseball practice after school each day, so I'd usually hang around too, doing homework or killing time, and Nick would be gone when I got to the apartment. Things between us had gone from strained to snapped.

As had become habit, I checked to make sure Nick's truck was gone before approaching the apartment. I'd just set my bag down and was heading into the kitchen to grab a snack when I noticed someone sitting in the raggedy old recliner, facing straight at the door like he'd been waiting for me.

"Didn't expect to see me?" Nick planted his hands on the arms and rose to a stand.

I worked on slipping into the skin I'd jumped out of. "Your truck. It was gone."

"Yeah, I parked it down the street a ways."

"Why did you do that?" I asked.

Nick's brow lifted. "Because I figured it's what you've been using to know if I'm home or not." He was staring at me like he was expecting me to say something or admit something or . . . *something.* Did he know about Kel and me? If so, how? We'd been extra careful so this type of confrontation wouldn't happen.

I kept moving into the kitchen, eager for any distraction. The sound of Nick's boots followed me.

"About this past weekend . . . ," he started as I threw open the first cupboard.

"I know, I know," I said, coming up empty in the snack department. "I shouldn't have done that. It won't happen again."

Nick didn't say anything right away. I had to check to make sure he was still in the room. An expression that I read as confusion was pulling at his forehead. Then a long breath came from him. "You weren't the only one who did something they regret that night," he said, shaking his head. "It was wrong of me to go off on you the way I did." Nick concentrated on the linoleum of the kitchen like there was a script stuck to it he was reading from. "When I saw you with him, getting back so late . . . I lost my cool."

I closed the cupboard and turned around. "You lost your cool?" I echoed, crossing my arms.

Nick rubbed at the back of his head. "I lost a lot more than that, too," he added, motioning at me. "That's what happens when a dad finds his daughter with that kind of guy late at night. About to do what you two were." Nick was turning red as he cleared his throat.

"Kissing?" I rested into the counter. "We were about to kiss. That's all."

He sighed, concentrating. "Look, I'm willing to admit I messed up, but you've got to know you messed up too. You lied about where you were going and who you were going with. That's not okay, Quinn."

I shifted. "I—I—" I stammered. "You're right. I'm sorry."

He sniffed, seeming almost surprised by my apology. "This parenting thing . . . it's not something that comes naturally, contrary to popular opinion. Most days I think

I'm hurting you more than I'm helping." There was a pause. "No, most days I *know* I'm hurting more than I'm helping," he finished, turning to head for the door. "I'm sorry too, Quinn."

My throat bubbled with a sob. I didn't know what to think or what to say. Nick had just apologized to me, even though I'd clearly messed up. Mom would have been upset too if I'd skipped town all day with some boy she didn't know and got back well after midnight.

My stomach knotted next when I realized he trusted me. Even when I'd given him no real reason to. Even as I was sneaking behind his back with the very boy he'd told me to stay away from.

"Nick?" I called as he opened the front door. "How would you feel about having Kel over for dinner one night? So you could have a chance to actually meet and get to know him?"

His back stiffened. "I don't think that's a good idea, Quinn."

"It's not the worst idea either," I said, not about to let this go so easily. If Nick just had a chance to get to know the real Kel, I knew he'd see the same good qualities in him I did.

"Quinn—"

"Please," I whispered. "Please do this for me."

Whatever he'd been about to say didn't make it. Nick's mouth clamped shut, a grumble coming from deep in his chest. "Fine. One dinner."

"Thank you," I half shrieked.

"Yes to having dinner with him doesn't mean I'm saying

160

yes to my daughter dating him, you understand?" He gave me a no-nonsense look.

My feet shifted. "Understood."

"So you're sure you're okay with coming to my place and having dinner with Nick?" I basically blurted in the middle of the morning's make-out session before school.

Kel gave me an amused smirk, giving himself a moment to catch his breath. "Isn't that what I just said? Like not even five minutes ago?"

"Yeah, but, you know, I wanted to give you a chance to change your mind."

"And you think what we were doing in those few minutes after I said yes would give me a reason to change my mind?" At the same time he drew me to him, I could sense him holding his distance.

"Is that you implying I bribed you into agreeing to dinner?"

His finger curled beneath my chin, as his lips hovered above mine. "Whether that was bribery or gratitude, does it seem like I care?"

"No," I whispered, brushing the corner of his mouth. "It doesn't."

His mouth captured mine, deepening our kiss as my hands skimmed up the worn front of his sweatshirt. My head spun as my feet melted into the floor. Kissing him had this weird way of making me feel like I was flying at the same time I was sinking. I'd never felt anything like it before. I wasn't sure I ever would again.

Kel kissed like it was a last kiss, every time. He held nothing back.

An uneven breath rattled in his lungs when he pulled back a minute later. His thumb stroked my cheek as his eyes circled the small room. "I never knew I was such a big fan of theater."

My lips were still tingling from his embrace, the sensation spreading through the rest of my body. "Might not want to hang up your bat yet, Hamlet. Especially with you leading the district in home runs this season."

"Yeah, but baseball doesn't come with these kinds of perks."

When his mouth grazed my neck, a shiver scattered down my spine. "What perks?"

I felt his smile curve against my skin. "A very private prop closet."

With the way he was touching me, I had to really focus to verbalize anything that wasn't nonsensical. "From the smell of this place, that door gets opened a whole two times a year."

Kel inhaled against my jawline. "Hmm. I don't know. It doesn't smell so bad to me."

One of my hands dropped from his chest to land on my hip. "So I don't smell *so* bad. Just a little bit?"

"You know what I mean."

"And you're lucky you took a shower after early practice, because sweat, dirt, and grass aren't exactly fine odors either." Okay, so that was a lie—that scent trifecta might have been exactly my kind of thing.

When I went to tickle at his sides, he fell back a step into a large wood cutout of a pirate ship. A wince swept across his face.

"Oh gosh. Sorry. Are you okay?" I exclaimed, pulling his sweatshirt up his back where he'd first grabbed at. I don't know what I was expecting to find, but nothing prepared me for what I saw.

"I'm fine. Just hit my back weird." He attempted to yank his sweatshirt from my hand, but I held on tight.

"And what about this is fine?" I blinked at the smattering of bruises spread along his back, which could have led anyone to believe he'd been stampeded by a herd of horses.

His eyes found mine. All the warmth had bled from them. "Quinn. I'm fine."

When I brushed my fingers along one of the bigger bruises, his jaw ground as if he was bracing himself. "If you tell me you're fine one more time, I'm going to lose it," I said.

"Would you stop with all this overreacting stuff?" Kel pulled away from me, yanking his sweatshirt out of my hand. "God. Every time I make a face that comes close to pain, you feel the need to check every square inch of my body and grill me if you find the smallest bruise. It's getting old."

"And you might be the only human being on the planet who complains about someone showing their concern for you."

Kel grabbed his bag from the floor and headed from the room. "Yeah, well spare me your concern. I'm a big boy. I can take care of myself."

"I never said you couldn't," I said, following after him.

He spun on me. "That's exactly what you're saying every time you get on my case about this stuff."

"This stuff?" I blinked at him in disbelief. "Kel, it's like a team of elephants played soccer on your back."

He gave a sharp huff before storming away. "Spare me the theatrics."

The sound of the theater doors screeching closed sounded shortly after. "And here I thought you said you were such a big fan of theater," I said to an empty room.

Realize it's rarely ever about you.

So no big deal. Kel was just going to be coming over for dinner and sitting at the same table as Nick. What could possibly go wrong, right?

Or at least he was supposed to be if he hadn't changed his mind after our fight in the theater. After that, we'd avoided each other for the rest of the day. He was obviously upset with me, and to be honest, I was mad at him, too. All I'd done was try to show I cared, and he responded like I was accusing him of a crime. Maybe I should have rescheduled dinner for another night. One when the last words Kel and I had spoken to each other hadn't been heated.

But that was going on the assumption he wanted to see me again at all.

I checked the time as I finished slicing the tomato for the cheeseburgers I was making for tonight. Nothing like a thick patty of meat on a bun to keep a couple of guys focused on food instead of each other. Hopefully.

Nick was pretending to be distracted by the baseball game on television, but his attention kept roaming toward the door, his jawbone about to burst through his skin every time he did.

"You sure he's still coming? I'd understand if he was too scared to want to confront me."

I groaned silently as I layered slices of cheese onto the patties sizzling in the pan. "He's still coming," I said, wondering if my answer sounded as doubtful to Nick as it did to me.

"I can be a pretty intimidating guy." Nick glanced back at the kitchen, flexing his arm at me.

When he caught me fighting a smile, he grinned. "What? You saying I need to hit the gym and pump some iron?"

"Maybe you can start with adding something more to your lunch than just coffee and beef jerky. Baby steps to intimidation domination."

Nick grunted at that, right as a knock vibrated against the door.

My body went stiff, while Nick's went into motion.

He came.

Striding toward the door, Nick bounced his shoulders a few times, and I didn't miss the way he stretched to his full height before swinging the door open.

Kel stood on the other side, appearing as collected as someone could in this situation. He stuck his hand out but drew it back first to wipe it off on his jeans before extending it again. "Hi, Mr. Winters. Thanks for inviting me for dinner."

Nick's arms folded over his chest, still barricading the door with his body. "I didn't. Quinn did."

"Oh. Yeah." Kel's hand fell back to his side. "Well, thanks anyway, then."

"Nick," I grumbled under my breath.

He eventually stepped aside so Kel could come in.

"Hey." My shoulders relaxed when I saw him. Everything else tensed, though.

A smile pulled at his mouth, a look in his eyes that said our argument was behind him. Forgotten. Forgiven. I think I took my first full breath since yesterday morning.

"Hey." Kel kept one eye on Nick as he came toward me. "These are for you." When he held up a simple bouquet of flowers, Nick didn't make his throat-clearing subtle. "For both of you. As a way to say thanks for having me to dinner." Kel rested the flowers on a patch of empty counter. "My mom always used to say you should never show up to someone's place empty-handed."

I grabbed the closest thing to a vase Nick had in his cupboards: a water glass. "My mom said that too."

"Smart ladies." Kel seemed lost, like he wasn't sure what to do next. Going in for a hug, or, lord forbid, a kiss, would earn him a one-way ticket through the window compliments of Nick. So instead he just hovered in the small kitchen. "You need some help?"

"It's all done," I announced as I switched off the burners. "What do you want to drink?"

"If it helps narrow the choices, we have water. And orange juice." Nick's arms managed to cross even tighter. "That's all."

I shot Nick a quick glance, but he totally missed it.

"I'm good with water. Thanks." Kel snagged one of the glasses off the table and headed toward the faucet. "What do you guys want? I'll take drink duty."

"Quinn doesn't want whatever was being served at that abandoned car wash the other night. You might remember it: the place you took her, then left her, so she could get hauled out by a security guard. From the sounds of it, there was enough liquor confiscated to stock a minimart."

Kel turned off the water but stayed facing the window. "I don't drink, Mr. Winters. And Quinn didn't drink any of that stuff that night either."

"You don't drink as in the past twenty-four hours?"

"I don't drink as in ever." Kel slowly turned. "And I never will."

When Nick gave a huff of what was pretty obviously doubt, I shot him another look. This one he didn't miss so much as openly ignore.

"And I'm sorry about what happened to Quinn that night. All I want is to keep her out of harm's way, not put her right in the center of it." Kel wandered to the table, setting his glass down before reaching for the other two.

Nick was just opening his mouth when I finally caught his attention.

"Please," I mouthed, pausing in the middle of cheeseburger assembly.

He watched me for another moment, then exhaled.

"Fine," he mouthed back. "So. Kel." Nick's neck stiffened. "I hear you're one hell of a baseball player."

Kel's shoulder lifted as he filled the other glasses at the sink. "I'm okay."

"Word is you're better than okay."

"He leads the state in RBIs," I added briskly. Even Nick appeared impressed at that one—not that he'd ever say it. Instead he changed tactics.

"Did your dad teach you to play?"

A sharp grunt came from Kel. "Not even," he said. "I picked it up messing around with other kids in the neighborhood. Learned how to play catch in back alleys and hit a ball in abandoned lots. That kind of thing." Kel's face was calm, talking about baseball. "When I was nine, a coach for a Little League team saw me playing in a park one day and somehow managed to convince my mom to let me join. He even paid my team dues and got me real gear that hadn't been scavenged from a garage sale or a dumpster."

Nick took the first plate I'd finished prepping and brought it to the table. "That a local Little League team?"

"No, sir. It was a team down in Redding."

"How long you live in California for?"

My breathing was back to normal now that the two of them were carrying on a conversation that didn't indicate it would end in disaster.

"About two years."

"Where'd you go from there?"

"Oregon. Two years in Eugene, and one year in Portland, before making it to Washington."

"Been in Renton ever since then?"

Kel cleared his throat. "We were in Long Beach first, then Pasco, and *then* Renton."

Nick paused as he reached for the next plate ready for the table. "Your family in the military or something?"

"No." Kel stuffed his hands in the pockets of his baggy jeans. "We just move a lot."

I hurried and finished plating the third dinner and carried it to the table. Nick was encroaching on off-limits territory, and I needed to run interference if he inched any closer. Kel had yet to open up to me about much of his home life, and it didn't take a wizard to predict Nick would make even less headway.

"That's got to be hard on a kid." Nick's hands draped around the back of his chair, appraising Kel with what might have been sympathy. At least it wasn't contempt. Progress.

"You get used to it."

Once I set my plate down, I ran back for the flowers. "Take a seat. Dinner's ready," I said as I centered the arrangement on the table.

The two bodies on either side of me didn't move. Okay, so I guessed I'd go first.

Once I dropped into my chair and scooted up to the table, Kel followed. Nick remained standing.

"Thanks for the flowers. I think I forgot to say that earlier." I smiled at Kel as I unfolded my napkin into my lap.

"You put together a legit dinner." Kel motioned at his plate. "And all you got was flowers. I've got some making up to do."

A laugh slipped from me, but Nick visibly clenched at the exchange.

"You spend a lot of time in the principal's office, don't you?" Nick finally took a seat. "Seems whenever I show up to grab my paycheck or come in early for a shift, more times than not I see you in there."

Kel reached for the ketchup, shifting in his seat. "I probably spend more time than the average student inside that office."

"Why?"

Nick was back to ignoring my pleading looks.

"Skipping class mostly." Kel squirted a swirl of ketchup onto his bun before smashing it back onto his burger. "Sometimes because they want to make sure they're doing their due diligence."

The corners of Nick's eyes creased. "What does that mean?"

"It means they see my face beat to shit"—Kel winced—"sorry, *crap*, and so sometimes they feel the need to ask questions." Kel took a bite of his cheeseburger, which was promptly followed with an impressed glance my direction.

"And why does your face, or whatever else, get beat to crap?"

"Bad luck," Kel answered after he'd finished chewing.

"Bad luck?"

"Pretty much, yeah." Kel took a drink of his water, doing a better job at hiding his discomfort than I was. "And maybe I get in a few fights here and there too."

"Like the one you got in the night Quinn wound up with that nasty shiner on her cheek?" Nick's neck popped when he moved his head. Watching him was like waiting for someone to crack open a soda they'd just shaken the heck out of.

Kel picked at the Tater Tots on his plate. "That's right."

"So you're comfortable using your hands to do harm?" Nick sniffed. "Have you ever hit a girl?"

"What?" Kel's head snapped up. "No. Never."

"Nick . . . ," I warned.

Nick would not be detoured. "Why do you get in fights?"

Kel blew out a puff of air, glancing at the time on the clock. He'd barely been here ten minutes. "I don't know. Because I guess I don't see eye to eye with the person standing in front of me."

"And what happens if Quinn says or does something you disagree with?" Nick's hand thrust in my direction. "Is your solution going to be taking a swing at her?"

Kel's face fell. "God, no. I'd never ever hit a woman."

Nick reached for his burger, giving a little grumble. "You'll understand if I remain skeptical on that. I'm just the father of the young girl you're spending time with."

My fork clattered against my plate. "Nick, please. He's here for dinner, not an interrogation."

Nick waved his hand as he took a bite of his burger, eating it without really tasting it. Kel and I tried to get back to our dinners, but it was pretty obvious neither of us was into it either.

A few minutes of silence went by before Nick dropped his burger on his plate. "What would you do if you had a daughter who brought home a guy like you? Huh?"

Kel didn't reply for a long moment; then he rose from his seat. "Probably the same thing you're doing right now," he said, giving a quick check my way. "Thanks for dinner, Quinn. You're a hell of a good cook."

"You're leaving?" I eyed his mostly untouched dinner.

Kel shot a brief look at Nick before heading toward the door. "I think it's for the best."

My head whipped to Nick, waiting for him to apologize and tell Kel to stay. Nick kept his mouth glued shut.

I shoved from my seat and hurried after him. "Kel—"

"Thanks again," he replied, closing the door behind him.

My eyes welled as I stared at the door, just able to detect the echo of his footsteps thudding down the stairway. My disappointment transformed into rage.

"What was that?" Spinning on my heels, I didn't pause to regulate my tone.

"That was a father looking after his daughter. That's what that was," Nick said, his posture stiff.

"By grilling Kel like he was guilty of murder?" I was shaking from emotions, which made my voice wobble too. "And who are you to tell someone how to treat a woman? You left your wife and child all alone."

Nick suddenly burst from his chair, spinning around to face me. "I'm here now," he half shouted. "And you will not talk to your father like that again."

I stormed toward my room before the tears could fall. "Forgive me," I said, my tone toxic. *"Father."*

*Remember. French fries
are gluten-free.*

The following Monday, once I finally made it through the torrential downpour—seriously, how can one sky produce that much moisture?—and past security at the school's front entrance, I went off in search of Kel. After the disaster known as dinner, I needed to check in with him and apologize for Nick going all Overprotective Father on him. My shoes were so soaked, they made squishing, slurping noises as I moved through the halls, sounding more like suction cups than sneakers.

There were a few students milling around, hanging at lockers, but it was quiet compared to the rest of the day. I checked around to make sure no one was paying attention before ducking inside the theater. It was dark other than a few soft lights just barely illuminating the stage. I usually tried to make as little noise as possible as I moved through the set, but that was impossible to do with my dripping shoes.

Bending around the stage curtains, I rushed toward the prop room. This was usually the point Kel grabbed me from behind and all other sensory details besides him faded away.

But there was no sign of him.

"Kel?" I whispered into the dark. No answer.

My fingers fumbled for the switch.

"Kel?" I repeated once light flooded the room.

He wasn't here. It was the first time he hadn't been waiting for me since we'd discovered this place a few days earlier. No matter how early I arrived, he was always here first, waiting. For me.

After checking behind a few of the bigger props and boxes to make sure he wasn't hiding and hoping to scare me, I rested on the old piano bench and waited.

Eventually, I got nervous. I couldn't be tardy to first period again without an excuse. Nick would no doubt get a phone call alerting him of my absence, which would only raise more questions.

Flipping off the lights, I left with a disappointed sigh.

The halls were swarming when I exited the theater. I couldn't help scanning the crowds for one dark-haired boy with wild eyes towering above the rest. No sign of him.

Maybe he'd come down with a cold over the weekend or had an appointment or something.

Suddenly, I noticed a familiar face in the crowd, though not the one I had been searching for. I raced after him. "Ben!" I called weaving through the herd.

"What's up, Quinn?" Ben slowed to let me catch up, his eyes widening when he saw me. "You realize you're, like, soaking wet, right?"

"Yes, well, some of us are license-less." My sneakers were still making slurping sounds, but they were muffled thanks to the rest of the noise in the hall.

"I told you I'd pick you up in the mornings if you wanted. You're on my way." Ben high-fived one of the other baseball players as they passed.

"I know, and I appreciate it, but I like to walk—most days at least."

"Can't say I get the appeal." He gazed at the ends of my hair, which were dripping the last few drops of rain they'd soaked in on the way here.

"Have you seen Kel?" I blurted before he headed into his class.

Ben stopped, giving me one of those pointed stares I was familiar with coming from my friends. The Look of Suspicion. "Why? What do you want with Kel?"

"Ben—"

He cracked a smile, nudging me. "Don't worry. You don't have to stress about me busting your balls—or busting your *whatever*—to get intel about Kel. I haven't seen him. The team had a weight lifting session this morning and he didn't show. He must be home sick or something."

His answer didn't necessarily make me feel better, but I had to get to class or else I was going to be late. "Thanks, Ben."

"You bet," he called after me. "And, Quinn, maybe at least grab an umbrella next time!"

I managed to make it to PE by the last fraction of the bell, but my mind was totally somewhere else for the rest of the school day.

It was the first day Kel had missed in weeks, and I couldn't shake off that unsettled feeling in my stomach that something was wrong. I left school that afternoon with one destination in mind.

Kel still didn't like the idea of me going to his place. Other than that one time, I'd never been back inside his apartment.

Most of the time, he'd say his mom wasn't feeling well with some cold bug or backache and that he didn't want to bother her. Sometimes he'd say she'd worked a late shift and was sleeping. A few times he'd come up with nothing more creative than to say it just wasn't a good time. Kel didn't want me at his apartment, but that's exactly where I was going.

In the daylight, it wasn't so rough-looking, I thought as I approached the apartment complex. It was just more depressing than anything. Old people sitting alone on their patios with half-broken chairs, a couple of toddlers running around the patchily grassed yard in nothing but their diapers and T-shirts, food wrappers and bottles scattered around like it rained trash here instead of water.

Everyone ignored me.

My hand froze in front of the door. I took a breath and then I knocked.

I could hear footsteps moving behind it. I wasn't sure who would answer.

The door opened a crack, one dark eye blinking out at me.

"Kel?" My voice was a whisper.

He sighed when he saw me standing there, opening the door a little wider. "What are you doing here, Quinn?"

"I came to check on—" My voice cut off when I saw him. When I *really* saw him. My hand planted on the door, pushing it open a little wider. "What happened?" I looked at his face. "Oh my god . . ."

"I'm okay," he said, keeping me from shoving the door open any wider. "You should go."

"You are *not* okay," I cried, swallowing as I stared at his face. One eye was so swollen shut, it seemed like a lime was hiding under his eyelid. His lower lip was split open, a fresh scab sealing it up. He was holding his left arm funny, his wrist showing signs of swelling and bruising. There was still a splatter of blood soaked into his faded gray sweatshirt, though from the way it had streaked, I could tell that in his attempt to clean it, he'd only smeared the blood around.

"You need to go." Kel checked over his shoulder. "Now."

I braced my other hand against the door and grounded my feet, taking all my strength to keep him from closing it. "Not until you tell me what happened."

In the background, I could hear noises coming from the apartment.

"Is that your mom?" I asked, craning my head to try to see inside. He adjusted himself, blocking my view. "Has she seen you like this? Are you going to at least let her take care of you, since you won't let me in?"

"What are you even doing here?" Kel pulled his hoodie up over his head with his free hand, but it made him wince doing so. He'd done something to his wrist.

"You didn't come to school. You missed practice. I

wanted to apologize for the most hostile dinner in the history of ever." He kept staring at me. I continued, "Forgive me for being worried about you. If you had a phone that actually worked, I could have called instead." I gave up trying to heave the door open. Even with him looking like he'd gotten into a fight with a heavyweight wearing brass knuckles, I couldn't overpower him.

More noises echoed from the apartment. Something breaking, shattering. Kel shifted in front of the door, putting his hand on my shoulder and pushing me away. "I don't want you here. That's what I've been trying to tell you."

Tears sprang to the surface. "What's going on? What happened?"

Kel leveled his one good eye at me. "This isn't working."

Now that he was outside, his injuries became that much more obvious. Something, someone, had beaten the living crap out of him.

"I don't understand. . . ." My head shook, too much coming at me to sort through standing in the relentless rain. "I want to know what happened to you." For the millionth time, I wondered who he was getting into fights with. What was he getting into fights over? Why did he choose fighting instead of the countless other alternatives that were much less damaging?

"I don't want to close this door in your face, Quinn, but I will if you don't leave in two seconds." Kel's jaw worked, but even that motion seemed to cause him pain.

He was hurt and needed to get checked by a doctor this time. I wasn't going to let him convince me otherwise.

"I want to talk to your mom." I made another move for the apartment, trying to squeeze my way inside. Kel blocked

179

me, his good arm holding me at a distance. "I'm not leaving until I've made sure someone is going to take care of you."

Kel's good eye closed, a breath slipping past his lips. "I can take care of myself."

"Your present condition proves the opposite, Kel Remington." I shoved away his hand, frustrated I wasn't strong enough to get by him. Angry I wasn't strong enough to keep from crying because a boy was telling me to leave.

Disappointed that I just wasn't . . . *enough.*

To keep Mom alive, to keep Nick from bailing, to give Kel whatever it was he needed, to be the strong, confident person I needed myself to be.

I wasn't enough, and finally I accepted that that was what Kel was trying to tell me.

"You need to go." His voice was quieter, almost like he was able to see the defeat settling into my eyes.

"I—"

A muffled voice came from inside. It was gravelly, deep, the way a person sounded when they were waking up. A flash of panic moved across Kel's face as he moved me farther away from the door. "Dammit, Quinn," he breathed, his jaw locking at the same time as his eyes were swimming in fear. "I don't want you. How many times are you going to make me say it?"

He didn't have to shove me away with his hands this time. His words did more than his brute strength ever could. Tears started to fall, but there was no way he could tell with the rain beating down on my face. "You're just saying that," I said, glaring at him, trying to hate him. "You're so damn scared to let someone care about you that you push everyone away who gets close." I backed into the rain. "You're a coward." My voice shook, my finger stabbing in his direction. "You are a coward, Kel Remington."

My face contorted, but there was nothing to read on his face, the same void in his eyes. He was the shell I thought I'd cracked weeks ago, only to discover he'd barely let me chip the surface.

His gaze met mine for one brief moment before falling away. "I know," he said as he turned to move into the apartment.

"I hate you!" I shouted at his retreating form.

Kel's head gave a barely discernible nod. "Good." He closed the door behind him, leaving me outside in the pouring rain.

The rain had ended by the time I made it to Nick's apartment. It was getting dark by the time I got there, a handful of hours lost to aimless wandering while my brain struggled to put together what had just happened.

The pain was different than when Mom died. With Mom, I'd known it was coming. I'd had months to spread out the hurt. And when she finally took her last breath, I'd gone numb.

I wasn't numb now, though—nothing close. Kel's lash was an acute piercing; the kind of hurt that made it hard to breathe.

Nick was already at work when I got to the apartment. Thank god. We'd made a semi-amends after that fail of a dinner, but I needed to be alone right now.

I went straight to my bedroom, not bothering to peel off my wet clothes.

As I laid my head on the pillow, Mom's journal caught

my attention, resting on the nightstand where I'd left it after reading from it every night before bed.

Now I understood. Now I knew why she'd written what she had. Why she'd begged me in swoopy cursive and purple ink to stay away from Kel, or at least the kind of boy Kel was. Heartbreak. She'd been trying to save me from the pain that came when another human was reckless with your heart.

I should have known Mom couldn't give bad advice.

If I had listened, I wouldn't be feeling like this right now. Crushed. Small. Hopeless.

Kel was in trouble but refused to open up to me about it. Instead of trusting me with whatever it was he was going through, he pushed me away. Life with Nick, though it had become easier, was still awkward at times; that five-ton elephant in the room popping up between us whenever I began to think we were bonding.

Kel didn't want me anymore, and sometimes I still found myself questioning if Nick was only pretending to want me to make things easier. If he'd really wanted me, he wouldn't have stayed away for ten whole years, right?

Shoving off my bed, I dug out a file of paperwork I hadn't touched in weeks. Before the night was over, I'd finished filling in all the boxes.

Save twenty percent of what you make from your very first paycheck to your very last. Trust me, you'll thank me for this tip in fifty years.

Tuesday was a blur. From first period to sixth, I wasn't sure how I made it to all my classes in the right order at the right time, but my brain must have been cruising on autopilot. Kel was nowhere to be seen. Even though I told myself I wasn't looking for him, I was. He'd made himself clear yesterday that the two of us were over, but that didn't mean I didn't want to see him.

When Mr. Johnson asked me if I knew if Kel was all right after marking him absent for the second day in a row, I shrugged. The truth was too complicated. Kel wasn't all right. And neither was I.

The sadness from yesterday had morphed into anger today, pulsing like lava in my veins. Kel called it off because he was scared. Well, he didn't get to wash his hands of me that easily, not with just a few rushed words spoken through a half-open door. I wasn't letting him off the hook that quickly, I decided as I left school that afternoon.

My anger fueled my legs, making the trip to Kel's apartment faster than the first trip. The ground was still soggy from yesterday's rain, as though the earth itself was trying to swallow me, starting at my feet.

Today, I didn't pause before knocking when I made it to his apartment. I waited, not hearing anyone inside. I knocked again, this time louder. When I stopped to listen, a commotion stirred inside the apartment. Bottles clinked and objects fell somewhere deep within.

Finally, there was some fussing with the lock, and a male voice cursing inside, but not one I recognized. When the door flew open, I fell back a couple of steps. The smell of alcohol reached me first, followed by the sight of a creature looming in the doorway.

"What in the hell do you want?" The man was middle-aged and huge. He was twice the size of the average man and seemed to know just how to hold himself to appear bigger. Unshaven, reeking—this was *not* the person I'd expected to find waiting behind the door. My eyes flickered up to make sure I had the right apartment number.

"I asked you a question, girl." The man's thick arms crossed over his chest, stretching his stained, thin white tee to nearly its ripping point.

"Is Kel here?" My voice came out small and wispy-sounding.

The man grunted. "What do you want with Kel?"

"Is he here?" I peeked inside the apartment, but he took up almost the entire doorframe. Nothing could get out or in with the way he was standing there.

"No. I don't know where the hell he is," he answered, cracking his neck before spitting on his front patio.

My feet took me back another step. "Is his mom home?"

The man's chest lifted with his snort. "That's a good one." Another snort as he stretched his fingers, like they were stiff. "That bitch hasn't been home in five years. We don't exactly expect her to show up anytime soon."

My head began to spin, right there with my feet sinking in the mud. Who was this man? Where was Kel's mom?

What was happening?

"Who are you?"

He gave me a glower like I should back off already, but I couldn't. Not until the world made some semblance of sense again. "Excuse me?" he said, in a voice that was capable of reducing a person to cowering.

"Who are *you*?" I repeated, my voice wobbling on the last word.

His mouth twitched at the hint of fear in my voice. "I'm that son of a bitch's father. That's who I am."

The ground seemed to shift beneath my feet. Kel's father? He'd never said anything about his dad being in the picture. He'd never mentioned anything about . . .

And there they were.

The pieces I'd been missing. The puzzle finally came together. Kel's dad was flexing his fingers, drawing my attention to them.

My throat ran dry as a tremble scattered down my spine.

Swollen knuckles. A few split open and scabbed over.

My body started to carry me away, the realizations spiraling like a snowball.

"If you do see that little bastard, tell him to get his ass home. He took off with my damn truck again and there's going to be hell to pay." With that, Kel's father slammed the door in my face.

For the first time since Nick left us, I had a flicker of recognition for how lucky I was. My dad might have abandoned me, but he'd never put his hands on me.

My stomach twisted after the door slammed closed, giving me the feeling I was about to be sick. I wanted my mom. I wanted her words of wisdom and, especially, her soothing embrace. I wanted someone to cry with and someone to help me decide what to do with the knowledge I'd stumbled upon. The knowledge I could not keep to myself.

I needed *someone*.

And then I knew who I needed. It was the last person I would have guessed.

My feet moved before I'd made my decision, running until my lungs burned as much as my legs. After unlocking the apartment, I couldn't get inside fast enough. "Nick?" I called, choking on the emotions clawing at my throat. He wasn't in the kitchen or his makeshift room. I finally found him hovering inside my bedroom, clutching a stack of papers in his hand, staring at them like he couldn't make sense of what he was reading.

It took me one second to realize what he was holding. "What is this, Quinn?" Nick's head turned toward me as he lifted the papers.

My stomach dropped. "I can explain—"

"I think it's pretty self-explanatory." Nick thrust his other hand at the papers. "You're trying to emancipate."

He stared at me, waiting for a response. I wasn't sure what to say anymore. Or how to explain it.

"I thought I wanted to . . . ," I began, my backpack falling from my shoulders to the floor. "I wasn't sure. . . ."

"You've filled in all the paperwork. It seems like you're sure." Nick rubbed at his forehead as he paced the floor of my bedroom.

"I'm not." It escaped as a whisper, one so soft he couldn't hear it.

"What are you going to do on your own, Quinn? Where are you going to go?" His voice was agitated. "Why wouldn't you at least mention something like this to me? Do you think this is the easiest living situation for me? Do you think I know what I'm doing trying to raise a teenage girl?" He looked like he was about to cry or burst a blood vessel. Other than the night he'd found me with Kel, I'd never seen Nick express so much emotion.

"I don't know what to say," I said, my body shaking.

"You know what? You don't need to say anything. This clearly isn't working for you." Nick powered out of my room, throwing the papers down on the sofa table as he passed.

"Nick, wait," I blurted, but he cut me off before I could finish.

"You don't need me. You never have," Nick huffed as he kept going. "Might as well make it official."

"That's not true. You don't understand." *I do need you,*

I realized all at once. But those words stayed stuck in my throat.

"You're right. I don't understand. Not a darn thing when it comes to raising a fifteen-year-old girl." Nick slammed the door behind him, causing me to flinch.

I stumbled into my bed, not sure what I wanted anymore. So I cried until I'd gone through a lifetime's worth of sadness, because I never wanted to shed another tear again.

The sound of muffled footsteps woke me up. It was late, still dark. A check of my cell phone showed it was just before five in the morning. Nick was usually home around two and went to bed right after. He must have been up, restless after our fight.

I hadn't closed my door all the way, so I was able to just hear a rustling noise followed by footsteps, like items were being stuffed into a bag. Then, after a minute, the sound of keys jingling as Nick moved toward the door.

When I heard the familiar whine of the front door opening, my heart stopped. Where was he going? Why was he leaving?

Throwing the covers off, I padded from my bedroom, still dressed in my clothes from yesterday. My eyes were puffy from the tears and my throat felt like sandpaper.

I headed straight for the living room window that overlooked the sidewalk below. Nick's truck was out front, which was unusual since he usually parked it in the small lot beside the building. Nick emerged from the main entrance a few seconds later, two duffel bags slung over his shoulder.

A nauseous wave roiled in my stomach.

Before I knew it, I was running, barefoot and hair whipping behind me. "Nick!" I shouted once I hit the hallway, though I knew he couldn't hear me. "Nick!" I yelled again, hustling down the stairs.

My heart was beating erratically, panic filtering into my veins, as I blasted through the building's front door and into the cold mist.

I heard the engine roar. It was the same sound I'd heard the night he'd left. It was the sound of abandonment.

Not again. He couldn't be doing this to me *again*. Ten years later and yet here I stood, feeling the same helpless, crushed feelings I'd had as a five-year-old who'd watched her dad drive away that night.

As the truck inched away from the curb, a flash of pure panic shot through me.

"Dad!" My voice pierced the night, cutting through the fog and cold.

"Dad!" I hollered.

My vision was blurry, but I could see Nick's eyes in his rearview mirror. I saw his eyes find me, too.

The brake lights shone into the night as the truck crept back to the curb. Then the driver's door burst open and Nick rushed out, leaving the truck running in the street.

"Please don't leave me." My voice broke as I choked on a sob. "Please stay."

The corners of his eyes lined as he came around the truck. "I'm not going anywhere."

I sniffed. "Your bags. It's the middle of the night."

Suddenly, Nick seemed to realize what was happening. "You didn't think . . . ?" He paused when he was a few feet away. "That I'd do that to you again? When you're all by yourself now?"

My gaze went from him to the truck, where a couple of bags were tossed into the bed, the scene too familiar.

When I stayed quiet, he closed the last bit of space between us. "I am not leaving you, Quinn." His arms folded around me carefully, giving me the chance to pull away. "I will *never* leave you again."

My body shook when he said those words. Without realizing it, I'd been waiting to hear him say that to me ever since arriving.

I shuffled closer, letting my own arms find their way around him. It was strange and awkward at first, but once he tightened his arms around me, drawing me close the way I remembered he used to when I'd been a child, it all came rushing back.

Hugging my dad was a reflex I just needed to give myself time to relearn. I smiled when I felt the coarseness of his beard against the side of my forehead. Home. It was a part of it.

"I love you, kid," he breathed, giving one last squeeze before guiding me toward the door. "Let's get you inside before your toes freeze solid."

We only made it a few feet before I stopped. "Wait. Where *were* you going?"

Nick unlocked the entrance, keeping me close. "That can wait. You're the most important thing in my life."

"What can wait?" I asked as I moved inside the building. The tile wasn't any warmer than the sidewalk outside.

Nick took a breath. "Answers."

He climbed the stairs with me in silence, closing the apartment door behind us when we made it inside. "Go grab some warm clothes, and I'll brew us a pot of coffee. I've got to make one quick call before we talk, but I promised you answers, and you deserve to hear them. I'll only be a minute."

I went to my bedroom in search of socks, half listening in on the phone call he was making. It lasted only a few seconds, and I couldn't make much sense of it. Something about meeting someone in trouble.

When I padded my warm feet back toward the kitchen, all wrapped up in a cozy blanket, Nick was measuring coffee into the filter. "I'm sorry if I scared you, Quinn. Truth is, I was on my way to meet a guy I sponsor. Through AA." He paused, glancing briefly at me before getting back to making coffee. "His wife just kicked him out of the house and he was having a moment when turning toward the bottle seemed like the best option. I keep a couple of emergency bags packed with clothes and toiletries for exactly these kinds of situations."

"You're a sponsor? Doesn't that mean . . . ?"

"I went through the program myself?" Nick nodded. "I did. Ten years ago, to be exact." He pulled a couple of cups free and motioned at the little dining table. Nick waited for me to take a seat before dropping into another. His throat cleared, his hands going from the table to his lap like he wasn't sure what to do with them.

"Did your mom ever talk about why I left you two?"

His question caught me off guard. *These* answers. These were the ones I was finally going to have.

"Not really. She just said you were both young when you got pregnant and things were hard." I tucked the blanket tighter around me, looking across the table at a man who seemed as conflicted as I felt.

"That's true. It was hard having a baby when we were a couple of kids ourselves." He checked over at the coffeepot, licking his lips. "But that's not the reason I left."

I stayed quiet, waiting for him to continue.

"I left because I was afraid I'd hurt you. Both of you." Dad's hand ran through his silvering hair, sighing. "No, I *knew* I'd hurt you both if I didn't leave."

My teeth worked at my lip. I had my suspicions why he'd left and was eager to finally have those confirmed or denied.

"I was an alcoholic." It erupted from him suddenly, his expression suggesting he was relieved his secret was out. "I *am* an alcoholic," he continued, settling into his seat. "I stopped drinking ten years ago, but I'll always be an alcoholic. It's an addiction I'll live with for the rest of my life."

I stayed quiet, letting him continue.

"It got really bad that last year before I left. So bad I got pulled over for flying through a red light, and I was so trashed I didn't even remember getting in the truck." Dad rose from his chair, rubbing his palms down his pants. "All I could think about was what could have happened if you two had been in the truck with me." His hands braced over the sink as he stared outside, where the faintest glow of light was spreading. "I was scared of other ways I could hurt you and not have any damn idea I was doing it. I didn't know how to stop drinking, so I did the only thing I could think of to keep you both safe." His head drooped as he exhaled. "I left."

I focused on my breathing to keep myself centered.

"I never knew . . . ," I started.

"Your mom believed that was my secret to tell, not hers." He grabbed a spoon and unrolled the sugar bag. "We kept in touch all these years. You probably didn't know that."

I twisted in my chair toward him. "You did?"

"Emails mostly. A couple of phone calls." Dad scooped a few spoons of sugar into my cup. "She'd send me pictures of you every once in a while, drawings you made. I'd send money. Which your mother would always send back." He snorted, smiling to himself. "When she got sick, we talked about what would happen to you after—" He reached for the pot of coffee, clearing his throat. "She mentioned there were some family friends who you could go live with, but she also suggested you could come live with me."

By this point in the story, my throat was one giant ball. Talking was not an option.

"I jumped at the chance to have you in my life again, Quinn. Selfishly." He stirred my coffee before bringing it to me. "Your mom knew I'd been sober all this time, and I think she felt it might be good for you, to have a fresh start where I was concerned."

He took a sip from his mug. "It didn't take long before I realized I'd made the wrong decision for you. That you were miserable here and didn't want anything to do with

193

me. When I found the emancipation paperwork yesterday, it just confirmed my greatest fears." He flashed a sad smile. "It wasn't you I was mad at, yesterday. I was mad at myself. For letting you down, again."

My head shook. "I'm sorry. I should have told you about the emancipation. I just didn't know if I wanted to go through with it. I was . . . confused," I said, summing up what felt like my whole life at the moment.

"Whatever you decide, I'll support you." Dad took another drink. "If you have to go through with the emancipation and moving back to Leavenworth, I will help you in whatever way you need. I promised your mom I'd take care of you, and I will. Even if that means letting you go."

My hands wound around my cup, getting warm.

"I don't want to go anywhere." I glanced over at him, working on a smile. "This is where I belong."

He had to gaze away for a minute. I could just make out the shine in his eyes from the corners. "You will always have a home with me, no matter what." He sniffed. "And I promise I won't let anything hurt you again the way I did."

I was in the middle of taking a drink when it clicked. "That's why you didn't want me to be around Kel? Because you didn't want me getting hurt again?"

Dad took a slow sip of his coffee. "I didn't want you hanging around that boy because I saw too much of the young me in him. I didn't want what happened to your mom to happen to you."

My nose wrinkled. "Getting pregnant?"

His eyes rounded. "Well, not that either," he said, still

recovering from me dropping the P word. "But I was talking about a broken heart."

My teeth worked at my lip as I debated how to bring up what I needed to. This was Kel's secret, but he'd never tell it. And if I didn't, who would keep him safe?

"Dad?" I started. "I need your help."

More questions are answered
in silence than in words.

"**W**hat are we doing?" My voice was nearly shrill with nervousness as Dad's truck barreled down the street.

"*You* are going to wait in the truck, and *I* am going to knock on the door to get Kel." Dad's hands wrung up and down the steering wheel as he stared through the windshield.

"What if his dad's there?"

"I'll deal with it."

My pulse was pounding in my throat, adrenaline pulsing through the rest of my body. When Dad had told me we were going to go get Kel after breakfast, I was flooded with relief, followed quickly by dread.

"Are you sure you don't want me to go with you?" I almost pleaded now.

"I can manage."

"But Kel's dad is dangerous," I argued.

"I'll be fine," Dad asserted tensely. The discussion was over.

When we turned into the complex, I pointed at his apartment. "That's the one," I said.

Dad nodded, easing the truck up to the curb. "Rough area," he said, unbuckling. "I sure hope you never so much as thought about coming here by yourself." Dad's brow rose as I fidgeted in my seat.

"Kel told me not to. He never wanted me coming around."

He grumbled as he reached for the handle. "That's one point in that kid's corner," he said, stepping outside, the truck still running. "Wait here."

A nervous wave came over me thinking of him confronting Kel's dad. "What if you need something?"

"If things go wrong, you call the police. Do not leave this truck, understand?" He waited for me to nod my acknowledgment. "I'll be back in a minute."

I spun around in my seat so I could watch him through the passenger window. Dad took long, purposeful strides toward Kel's apartment, not appearing the least bit intimidated. He didn't hesitate to knock when he stopped in front of the apartment. Then I held my breath, and we both waited. The door opened.

It wasn't Kel standing on the other side either.

Dad said something to Kel's dad; Kel's dad responded with his middle finger. Dad moved in closer, his shoulders lifting as he said something else. From the truck, I could only hear every few words, but each one was getting louder.

Kel's dad suddenly burst out laughing, followed by a two-word reply that I couldn't help but hear, before he grabbed the doorknob to go back inside. Before the door could slam, Dad shouted Kel's name.

The arm came around so quickly it was a blur, Mr. Remington's fist landing square into Dad's jaw. I was flying from the truck and sprinting before Dad even hit the ground.

"Dad!" I shouted. "Are you okay?"

"Get back to the truck, Quinn!" he yelled, lifting his hand when he saw me. But I was not stopping; I was not staying anywhere.

There were certain things in life worth fighting for. And fighting against.

"Where's Kel?" I shouted as I braked to a stop in front of Mr. Remington.

"I told you yesterday to stay away from here, girl. Don't make me teach you the same lesson I just taught your daddy."

Behind me, Dad was still shaking off the hit, like he was trying to wake himself up from a dream. "You call that a 'lesson'?" he huffed, struggling to get up.

Mr. Remington moved to get around me, but I leapt in his way, blocking his path. His dark eyes dropped to me.

"Where's Kel?" I repeated, trying to keep from trembling.

"Get out of my way." His breath reeked of alcohol, making my stomach clench.

I planted my feet even more firmly in place. "No."

His dark eyes flashed. "Suit yourself."

He moved fast for a man his size; his arm swung before I could even begin to react.

I braced for the hit when someone dove in front, thrusting me aside and deflecting the blow. Kel stood between me and his dad, planting himself in front of me protectively.

"Not her." Kel's voice was unrecognizable, his back quivering. "Not. Her." Kel spit the words, throwing his dad's arm away.

Something flashed across Mr. Remington's face—was it doubt? fear?—but then the storm of anger returned. "What did you just say to me?"

"You heard me."

"I don't think I did." Mr. Remington advanced toward his son, but Kel drove his shoulder into his dad, shoving him into the apartment complex wall. His dad's arm swung again, but Kel ducked, his own fist connecting with his dad's cheek.

Mr. Remington fell into the wall again, his legs buckling beneath him. He crashed to the ground with a pathetic whimper.

Kel hovered above him, shaking so hard his teeth were practically chattering. "Did you hear me now?" he shouted. "You will not touch her! I won't let you!"

Dad was finally up at this point. I couldn't look away from the scene playing before me, one of roles being reversed and Kel realizing all at once that he was strong. Stronger than he'd thought. Stronger than his father.

"Kel." Dad placed a hand on his shoulder. "Come on, son. Let's go."

Kel flinched when he felt Dad's hand but relaxed when he saw who it was standing behind him. When his eyes landed on me, I wanted to cry because I finally understood who he was.

Not a coward, but the strongest person I'd ever met.

I lifted my hand to Kel's cheek, a bruise already blooming on his skin. His eyes closed as my hand cupped around his face. "I was just trying to protect you," he breathed. "From all of this."

"You did, Kel," I said. "You did." I glanced back at his dad, still sprawled on the ground outside his apartment. He didn't seem so large from this vantage point. "And you will not touch him again," I said, my voice as calm as I'd ever sounded as I glared down at the pitiful creature below me. "I won't let you."

Who ever said life was a serious affair?

The rain decided to finally give us a break. It made us wait until May, but there was something more special about the sun and blue skies when a person had endured months of drizzle and gray. The storms defined the calm, but the calm defined the storms, too. They were tied to each other.

"It's not fair to the other teams, you know?" Dad called over at Kel as he rounded the fence at the end of the baseball game.

He had dirt and sweat streaked all over his face and uniform, and had just played nearly three hours in eighty-degree heat, but he was smiling. "What's not fair?"

"That they have to play you." Dad eyed the scoreboard, which was heavily one-sided.

"Good game, Kel," Allison and Madeline sang as they climbed down from the bleachers, where we'd been camped together, sucking down frozen lemonades and downing licorice like it was our life's calling.

"Thanks." Kel waved, stopping in front of me with an all-too-familiar smirk in place. "So?"

My eyes lifted as I smiled. "I think that third home run you were off a foot or two from where I pointed."

"Foot or two, my ass. My *butt*," Kel edited when Dad cleared his throat.

"All right, you two. You can continue giving each other a hard time in the truck." Dad climbed down the bleachers. Kel extended his hand so I could step down onto the grass too.

"The Pie Shack?" I asked, our usual celebratory stop.

"We've got an errand to run." Dad chuckled when he saw both Kel's and my faces take a downward turn. "But the Pie Shack after." He added, "And *then* homework tonight."

I grumbled. Kel didn't. "It's Saturday. We can do homework tomorrow."

"Why put off to tomorrow what you can finish today?" Dad said, like he was reciting a speech to a crowd of people. "How am I doing with this parenting thing, by the way?"

"A little too good," I teased as we wandered toward the parking lot.

"Hey, Remington!" one of Kel's teammates called from across the field. "All of us are meeting at Ben's tonight to celebrate the win. You going to make an appearance?"

Kel lifted our combined hands. "Sorry. I already have plans."

I smiled over at him. We didn't really have plans. But

after a long week of school and practice and homework, it was nice to have a few hours to do nothing together.

"Whipped," his teammate hollered, making a whipping motion.

Kel pointed at him, laughing. "Jealous."

His teammate motioned at me before jogging over to his teammates. "Guilty."

When we reached the truck, Dad threw Kel's bag into the bed while Kel dusted himself off and changed out of his cleats.

"Where are we going?" I asked after we all piled in.

Dad's face lit up as he backed out of the parking space. "It's a surprise."

Kel's arm found its way around me as we left the lot, my head falling to his shoulder. The past couple of months had flown by, and the end of the school year was fast approaching. Somehow, we'd found a way to make our living arrangement work. Three very different people living in one very cramped space presented a number of challenges—especially when two of those people were teens in a relationship—but we'd surprised ourselves, all of us.

It didn't hurt that Dad had switched from working nights to days.

Before long we turned down a few side streets, barely a mile away from the school. "Do you have to make a house call?" I guessed, knowing the few guys Dad sponsored could keep him busy as they continually worked on their sobriety.

Dad had a silly grin on his face. "Of sorts."

I glanced over at Kel for any clues, but he seemed as lost as I was.

"Have you gotten your court date for your emancipation hearing yet?" Dad asked Kel when he braked at a stop sign, waiting for a few cars to go through the intersection.

"Not yet. They say within sixty days after turning in the paperwork, so hopefully soon."

Dad looked over at Kel. "And your dad hasn't changed his mind about contesting it?"

Kel snorted. "No. To contest it would mean he actually gave a damn . . . a *darn*."

Dad's eyes narrowed as he stared through the windshield. "His loss," he muttered, before adding, "Nice you had someone who knew a little something about the general process. . . ." Dad nudged me.

"Definitely came in handy." Kel chuckled, staring through the window with me as we tried to guess where we were going.

After the day we showed up at Kel's apartment, he'd gone back only once: to serve the emancipation papers. Dad informed the school about the situation, and Kel and I had worked together to file the paperwork in record time. Kel now had a part-time job and had opened a bank account, so we were just waiting for the final approval.

Dad eased the truck up to a curb in a residential area. When he turned off the truck and opened the door, Kel and I both shot him a confused look.

"Where are we?" I asked.

Dad blinked at me like that should have been obvious. "We're here," he answered with a shrug.

Kel opened the door and helped me crawl down.

"Where's here?" I asked as Dad led us around the front

of a restored bungalow. Without a word, Dad pointed to the sign I'd missed when we'd first pulled up. It read, SOLD.

"Home," Dad said, beaming like a fool. "We're home."

My mouth fell open as I spun to view the cute little house with new eyes. "No. Way."

Dad leaned in, bumping his shoulder to mine. "Way."

Kel came up beside me, staring at the house with the same kind of surprise and awe.

"You bought this?" I said, blinking to make sure everything I was seeing was still there.

Dad grinned. "I've been saving up for years. I was just waiting for the right time. It's got a finished basement, too, which works especially well for our current needs." He reached over and patted Kel's shoulder.

"It's beautiful." My eyes welled with tears, happy ones, the only kind I'd cried the past couple of months.

There was a yard stretching from the front into the back, where I could already picture hanging a hammock from the two large maple trees. There were a ton of windows that would let in light, and character had been built into every detail of the home. It all came into focus suddenly, and there were birds chirping and children laughing and the smells of barbecuing—there was life all around me. I couldn't have imagined a better place to spend the last few years before leaving for college.

I clapped my hands. "When do we get to move in?"

"Tomorrow," Dad answered. "Why do you think I said you two had to finish your homework tonight? We're going to be busy tomorrow."

I threw my arms around Dad, hugging him hard.

"Before you get too excited"—Dad turned to face Kel and me once I let him go, a stern line stretched across his forehead—"there will be an alarm system for both the upstairs and basement apartments, and I'll be enforcing strict rules about curfew." Dad was staring straight at Kel. "She might be your girlfriend, but she was my daughter first. My house, my rules."

Kel raised his hands. "Your house, your rules, Mr. W."

My arm linked behind Dad, the other behind Kel. We stood there for a minute, staring at our future in physical form. "*Our* house."

Dad chuckled under his breath. "Okay, our house," he said, then added, "But still my rules."

The right time is right now.

A happy ending. A new beginning. That's what today was about.

School had wrapped up last week, and both Kel and I had both done well. I'd managed to squeak out all A's despite all the changes, and Kel had worked his butt off to get his grades to C's and even a couple of B's. Kel said it was thanks to all my tutoring, but I knew it was way more than that. He'd worked hard and he'd decided to care. The forty hours of tutoring credit I'd turned in last week might not have hurt, but those hours had been as beneficial to me as they had to him. Being needed, making a difference . . . turns out those weren't such lame clichés.

Despite my sophomore year holding some of the lowest lows in my life, it had some of the highest highs as well.

Today feels like something of a rebirth, I thought as I made that grassy walk up the hill. I had a bouquet of sunflowers clutched in my hand—her favorite—and the journal in my other.

It was a beautiful day in Leavenworth, the kind that made you dare to hope.

The cemetery was quiet, other than the sparrows chattering in the bushes lining the fence. The last time I'd visited, I'd watched my mom being lowered into the ground, feeling like part of me was going with her.

I felt alive again. Brought back by the people who loved me and the ones I loved in return.

Her gravestone shone in the sun, the slight pink hue of the granite glowing brighter in this kind of light.

Sarah Marie Winters, I read. *October 12, 1984–February 8, 2019. Beloved friend and mother.*

The tears were already spilling as I crouched down beside her grave.

Taking time to arrange the sunflowers just right, I settled the journal in my lap. I'd read her very last entry a couple of days ago, and with it a weight had been lifted. All the advice she'd given me in life, all the wisdom she'd penned onto paper, her final piece of guidance was this: live my life how I best see fit. That was it. That was all.

That was enough.

"Hey, Mom. It's me. Sorry it took so long for me to get here." I paused, having to take a slow breath. "Thank you for the journal. Thank you for everything you taught me. I know Kel isn't who you imagined for me. To be honest, this life isn't what I pictured either. I always thought you'd be by my side." My fingers curled around the edge of the notebook.

"But I still feel you guiding me and cheering me on. And Kel is a great guy. So I'm taking your advice. I'm breaking the rules and following my heart. I'm choosing *love*. Because I know that's what you would've done."

My hand lifted to her headstone, letting the warmth radiating from it pass through me. She was here, after all. Maybe not in physical form, but in other ways. The sun on my back. The bird's song. The cool grass tickling my legs. She was everywhere, but most especially, she was in my heart.

"Quinn Bee?" My dad's voice came from behind me, soft and unsure.

Sniffing, I wiped my face and rose from the ground. "I'm good," I said, waving him forward.

Muffled footsteps moved through the grass toward me, Dad's arm draping over my shoulders as he studied Mom's grave for the very first time. His eyes were red rimmed.

Glancing over my shoulder, I felt my face relax when I saw Kel standing there, waiting a ways off. "It's okay." I waved him toward us. "I promise I'm done melting down. For now."

He moved closer, seeming unsure. "I just wanted to give you time, some space."

My hand found his when he stopped beside me. "I've had all the time and space I need."

Kel's hand warmed mine as he stared down at my mom's grave. "She'd be proud, you know?"

My head nodded. "I know."

"I'm proud too." Dad nudged me before looking over at Kel. "I'm proud of you *both*." Wiping at his eyes all quick-like, Dad pulled something from his pocket as he took a few steps forward and kneeled at Mom's grave. He set it down on the grave marker, leaving his hand there for a moment while he said his own silent words to her. Then he rose and rejoined Kel and me.

On her name, I saw, he'd left a worn golden band. His wedding ring. He hadn't had a proper chance to say goodbye yet either.

We stood like that for a few minutes, all of us together.

Ultimately, it was Dad who broke the silence, bumping me with his arm. "We've got a birthday party to get to sometime, you know?"

I smiled, excited to see my old friends and eat cake until I gave myself a stomachache. "I'm coming. Just one more minute."

Dad patted my back before turning to leave. Kel lingered for another moment, leaning in to kiss the corner of my mouth. "Happy birthday, Quinn." Then he nuzzled my neck, making me laugh, before jogging to catch up with my dad.

I stood there for a moment, smiling. "Bye, Mom," I whispered, blowing her a little kiss. Then I turned to catch up with the two people in front of me, waiting.

"Hey, Dad?" I called once I'd caught up, linking my hand into Kel's.

"Hey what?"

"Why do fish live in salt water?" I asked, keeping a straight face.

The corners of his mouth lifted. "I don't know. Why?"

"Because pepper makes them sneeze."

Dad chuckled, shaking his head. "I think our jokes need some work. That was lame."

"What? Like that cheetah jungle one of yours was so

much better?" I teased, walking around to the front of the truck. Kel was waiting with the door already open. The driver's door. I'd gotten my license first thing this morning.

Before climbing in, I turned to stare at the spot where the sunflowers were brimming and the faint sparkle of an old wedding band could be seen.

"You ready to head to the party?" Kel asked.

I took a deep breath and closed my eyes. "I'm ready," I said at last, crawling inside the truck.

His hand found mine as I turned the key in the ignition. "I'm ready too."

I stared through the windshield, smiling at the thought of all that was waiting up ahead. My hands moved to the steering wheel as my foot pressed the accelerator, moving us all forward. "Then let's go."

ACKNOWLEDGMENTS

This book was a unique challenge to write in so many ways. I wanted to create a love story about two broken individuals who come to realize that, sometimes, growth sprouts from the fractured places. This story would not be what it is without the team that was committed to giving Quinn and Kel the book they deserved.

To my fearless editors, Phoebe Yeh and Elizabeth Stranahan. I am eternally grateful for your dedication to making my stories better. Your commitment to and passion for young adult literature is evident in every book I've had the privilege to work with you both on. I thank you for all of your time and advice, and for challenging me to become a better writer with each revision.

Thank you to my agent, Jane Dystel, for her tireless work ethic. I'm grateful to have such a professional, committed agent on my side.

To the book bloggers who give so much of themselves to spread the word of books: you all inspire me. To write better. To be better. To *do* better. You give so much to the book world without expecting anything in return. Thank you for continuing to read and share your love of books.

To my husband and daughter: my loves, my life. You are my reasons for everything.

To my family and friends, from so many different walks of life: Every day I'm grateful for the remarkable people who have been brought into my life. Your vulnerability, support, and love mean more than this writer could ever put into words. I love you all.

Last, to all of you readers out there: thank you for letting this bookworm live her dream. Never settle for anything less than yours.

ABOUT THE AUTHOR

Nicole Williams is the *New York Times* bestselling author of *Crash, Clash,* and *Crush,* and numerous other books, including the young adult novels *Trusting You & Other Lies,* which *Booklist* called "a charming summer romance," and *Almost Impossible,* which *SLJ* praised as "a fun and relatable summer read for fans of Sarah Dessen and Jenny Han."

A Spokane native, Nicole loves sunny days and happy endings. She lives with her husband and daughter, who turn her world upside down every day and take her on the best adventures.

authornicolewilliams.com